Goosebumps

MONSTER BLOOD

...d
...he stairs, leaning against the banister and taking the stairs three at a time. Then, running full-out, he practically flew to the dog run at the back of the garden.

"Trigger! Hey—Trigger!" he called.

Halfway across the back garden, Evan could see that something was wrong.

Trigger's eyes were bulging. His mouth was wide open, his tongue flailing rapidly from side to side, white spittle running down his chin, hair onto the ground. . . .

As Evan reached the dog run, Trigger's eyes rolled back, and the dog's legs collapsed under him, his stomach still heaving, the air filled with his loud, hideous gasps.

Evan's bought some really *cool* fake monster blood from a toy shop while staying with his creepy Aunt Kathryn. But soon Evan realizes that there's *more* to this monster blood than meets the eye—much more! In fact the stuff's growing so quickly it's getting *out of control!*

MONSTER BLOOD

R.L. STINE

Hippo

Scholastic Children's Books,
Scholastic Publications Ltd,
7-9 Pratt Street, London NW1 0AE, UK

Scholastic Inc.,
555 Broadway, New York, NY 10012-3999, USA

Scholastic Canada Ltd,
123 Newkirk Road, Richmond Hill,
Ontario, Canada L4C 3G5

Ashton Scholastic Pty Ltd,
PO Box 579, Gosford, New South Wales,
Australia

Ashton Scholastic Ltd,
Private Bag 92801, Penrose, Auckland,
New Zealand

First published in the US by Scholastic Inc., 1992
First published in the UK by Scholastic Publications Ltd, 1994

ISBN 0 590 55307 0

Typeset by Contour Typesetters, Southall, London
Printed by Cox & Wyman Ltd, Reading, Berks.

"I don't want to stay here. Please don't leave me here."

Evan Ross tugged his mother's hand, trying to pull her away from the front step of the small, pebble-dashed house. Mrs Ross turned to him, an impatient frown on her face.

"Evan—you're twelve years old. Don't act like a baby," she said, freeing her hand from his grasp.

"I *hate* it when you say that!" Evan exclaimed angrily, crossing his arms in front of his chest.

Softening her expression, she reached out and ran her hand tenderly through Evan's curly, carrot-coloured hair. "And I *hate* it when you do that!" he cried, backing away from her, nearly stumbling over a broken paving stone in the path. "Don't touch my hair. I hate it!"

"Okay, so you hate me," his mother said with a shrug. She climbed up the two steps and

1

knocked on the front door. "You've still got to stay here till I get back."

"Why can't I come with you?" Evan demanded, keeping his arms crossed. "Just give me one good reason."

"Your trainer lace is untied," his mother replied.

"So?" Evan replied unhappily. "I like 'em untied."

"You'll trip," she warned.

"Mum," Evan said, rolling his eyes in exasperation, "have you ever seen *anyone* trip over their trainers because the laces were untied?"

"Well, no," his mother admitted, a smile slowly forming on her pretty face.

"You just want to change the subject," Evan said, not smiling back. "You're going to leave me here for weeks with a horrible old woman and—"

"Evan—that's *enough!*" Mrs Ross snapped, tossing back her straight blonde hair. "Kathryn is not a horrible old woman. She's your father's aunt. Your great-aunt. And she's—"

"She's a total stranger," Evan cried. He knew he was losing control, but he didn't care. How could his mother do this to him? How could she leave him with some old lady he hadn't seen since he was two? What was he supposed to do here all by himself until his mother got back?

2

"Evan, we've discussed this a thousand times," his mother said impatiently, pounding on his aunt's front door again. "This is a family emergency. I really expect you to cooperate a bit more."

Her exact words were drowned out by Trigger, Evan's cocker spaniel, who stuck his head out of the back window of the rented car and began barking and howling.

"Now *he's* giving me a hard time, too!" Mrs Ross exclaimed.

"Can I let him out?" Evan asked eagerly.

"I think you'd better," his mother replied. "Trigger's so old, we don't want him to have a heart attack in there. I just hope he doesn't terrify Kathryn."

"I'm coming, Trigger!" Evan called.

He jogged to the gravel drive and pulled open the car door. With an excited yip, Trigger leapt out and began running in wide circles around Kathryn's small, rectangular front garden.

"He doesn't *look* like he's twelve," Evan said, watching the dog run, and smiling for the first time that day.

"See. You'll have Trigger for company," Mrs Ross said, turning back to the front door. "I'll be back from Atlanta in no time. A couple of weeks at the most. I'm sure your dad and I can find a house in that time. And then we'll be back before you know it."

"Yeah. Sure," Evan said sarcastically.

The sun dipped behind a large cloud. A shadow fell over the small front garden.

Trigger wore himself out quickly and came panting up the walk, his tongue hanging nearly to the ground. Evan bent down and patted the dog's back.

He looked up at the grey house as his mother knocked on the front door again. It looked dark and uninviting. There were curtains drawn over the upstairs windows. One of the shutters had come loose and was resting at an odd angle.

"Mum—why are you knocking?" he asked, shoving his hands into his jeans pockets. "You said Aunt Kathryn was totally deaf."

"Oh." His mother's face reddened. "You got me so upset, Evan, with all your complaining, I completely forgot. Of *course* she can't hear us."

How am I going to spend two weeks with a strange old lady who can't even hear me? Evan wondered glumly.

He remembered eavesdropping on his parents two weeks earlier when they had made the plan. They were sitting opposite each other at the kitchen table. They thought Evan was out in the back garden. But he was in the hall, his back pressed against the wall, listening.

His father, he learned, was reluctant to leave Evan with Kathryn. "She's a very stubborn old

4

woman," Mr Ross had said. "Look at her. Deaf for twenty years, and she's refused to learn sign language or to lip-read. How's she going to look after Evan?"

"She took good care of you when *you* were a boy," Mrs Ross had argued.

"That was thirty years ago," Mr Ross protested.

"Well, we have no choice," Evan heard his mother say. "There's no one else to leave him with. Everyone else is away on holiday. You know, August is just the worst month for you to be transferred to Atlanta."

"Well, excuuuse me!" Mr Ross said sarcastically. "Okay, okay. Discussion closed. You're absolutely right, dear. We have no choice. Kathryn it is. You'll drive Evan there and then fly down to Atlanta."

"It'll be a good experience for him," Evan heard his mother say. "He needs to learn how to cope under difficult circumstances. You know, moving to Atlanta, leaving all his friends behind—that isn't going to be easy on Evan either."

"Okay. I said okay," Mr Ross said impatiently. "It's settled. Evan will be fine. Kathryn is a bit weird, but she's perfectly harmless."

Evan heard the kitchen chairs scraping across the lino, indicating that his parents were getting up, their discussion over.

5

His fate was sealed. Silently, he had made his way out the front door and round to the back garden to think about what he had just overheard.

He leaned against the trunk of the big maple tree, which hid him from the house. It was his favourite place to think.

Why didn't his parents ever include *him* in their discussions? he wondered. If they were going to discuss leaving him with some old aunt he'd never seen before, shouldn't he at least have a say in the matter? He learned all the big family news by eavesdropping from the hallway. It just wasn't fair.

Evan pulled a small twig off the ground and tapped it against the broad tree trunk.

Aunt Kathryn was weird. That's what his dad had said. She was so weird, his father didn't want to leave Evan with her.

But they had no choice. No choice.

Maybe they'll change their minds and take me to Atlanta with them, Evan thought. Maybe they'll realize they can't *do* this to me.

But now, two weeks later, he was standing in front of Aunt Kathryn's grey house, feeling very nervous, staring at the brown suitcase filled with his belongings, which stood beside his mother on the step.

There's nothing to be afraid of, he assured himself.

6

It's only for two weeks. Maybe less.

But then the words popped out before he'd even had a chance to think about them: "Mum—what if Aunt Kathryn is evil?"

"Huh?" The question caught his mother by surprise. "Evil? Why would she be evil, Evan?"

And as she said this, facing Evan with her back to the house, the front door was pulled open, and Aunt Kathryn, a large woman with startling black hair, filled the doorway.

Staring past his mother, Evan saw the knife in Kathryn's hand. And he saw that the blade of the knife was dripping with blood.

Trigger raised his head and began to bark, hopping backwards on his hind legs with each bark.

Startled, Evan's mother spun round, nearly stumbling off the front step.

Evan gaped in silent horror at the knife.

A smile formed on Kathryn's face, and she pushed open the screen door with her free hand.

She wasn't anything like Evan had imagined. He had pictured a small, frail-looking, white-haired old lady. But Kathryn was a large woman, very robust, broad-shouldered, and tall.

She wore a peach-coloured housecoat and had straight black hair, pulled back and tied behind her head in a long ponytail that flowed down the back of the dress. She wore no make-up, and her pale face seemed to disappear under the striking black hair, except for her eyes, which were large and round, and steely blue.

8

"I was slicing beef," she said in a surprisingly deep voice, waving the blood-stained kitchen knife. She stared at Evan. "You like beef?"

"Uh . . . yeah," he managed to reply, his chest still fluttery from the shock of seeing her appear with the raised knife.

Kathryn held open the screen door, but neither Evan nor his mother made any move to go inside. "He's big," Kathryn said to Mrs Ross. "A big boy. Not like his father. I used to call his father Chicken. Because he was no bigger than a chicken." She laughed as if she had cracked a funny joke.

Mrs Ross, picking up Evan's suitcase, glanced uncomfortably back at him. "Yeah . . . he's big," she said.

Actually, Evan was one of the shortest kids in his class. And no matter how much he ate, he remained "as skinny as a spaghetti noodle," as his dad liked to say.

"You don't have to answer me," Kathryn said, stepping aside so that Mrs Ross could get inside the house with the suitcase. "I can't hear you." Her voice was deep, as deep as a man's, and she spoke clearly, without the indistinct pronunciation that some deaf people have.

Evan followed his mother into the front hallway, Trigger yapping at his heels. "Can't you keep that dog quiet?" his mother snapped.

"It doesn't matter. She can't hear it," Evan replied, gesturing towards his aunt, who was heading for the kitchen to put down the knife.

Kathryn returned a few seconds later, her blue eyes locked on Evan, her lips pursed, as if she were studying him. "So, you like beef?" she repeated.

He nodded.

"Good," she said, her expression still serious. "I always cooked beef for your father. But he only wanted pie."

"What kind of pie?" Evan asked, and then blushed when he remembered Kathryn couldn't hear him.

"So he's a good boy? Not a troublemaker?" Kathryn asked Evan's mother.

Mrs Ross nodded, looking at Evan. "Where shall we put his suitcase?" she asked.

"I can tell by looking at him that he's a good boy," Kathryn said. She reached out and grabbed Evan's face, her big hand holding him under the chin, her eyes examining him closely. "Good-looking boy," she said, giving his chin a hard squeeze. "He likes the girls?"

Still holding his chin, she lowered her face to his. "You've got a girlfriend?" she asked, her pale face right above his, so close he could smell her breath, which was sour.

Evan took a step back, an embarrassed grin crossing his face. "No. Not really."

"Yes?" Kathryn cried, bellowing in his ear. "Yes? I *knew* it!" She laughed heartily, turning her gaze to Evan's mother.

"The suitcase?" Mrs Ross asked, picking up the bag.

"He likes the girls, huh?" Kathryn repeated, still chuckling. "I could tell. Just like his father. His father always liked the girls."

Evan turned desperately to his mother. "Mum, I can't stay here," he said, whispering even though he knew Kathryn couldn't hear. "Please —don't make me."

"Hush," his mother replied, also whispering. "She'll leave you alone. I promise. She's just trying to be friendly."

"He likes the girls," Kathryn repeated, leering at him with her cold blue eyes, again lowering her face close to Evan's.

"Mum—her breath smells like Trigger's!" Evan exclaimed miserably.

"I'm going to bake you a pie," Kathryn said, tugging at her black ponytail with one of her huge hands. "Would you like to roll out the dough? I'll bet you would. What did your father tell you about me, Evan?" She winked at Mrs Ross. "Did he tell you I was a scary old witch?"

"No," Evan protested, looking at his mother.

"Well, I am!" Kathryn declared, and once again burst into her deep-throated laugh.

Trigger took this moment to begin barking ferociously and jumping on Evan's great-aunt. She glared down at the dog, her eyes narrowing, her expression becoming stern. "Look out or we'll put *you* in the pie, doggie!" she exclaimed.

Trigger barked even harder, darting boldly towards the tall, hovering woman, then quickly retreating, his stub of a tail whipping back and forth in a frenzy.

"We'll put him in the pie, won't we, Evan?" Kathryn repeated, putting a big hand on Evan's shoulder and squeezing it till Evan flinched in pain.

"Mum—" he pleaded when his aunt finally let go and, smiling, made her way to the kitchen. "Mum—please."

"It's just her sense of humour, Evan," Mrs Ross said uncertainly. "She means well. Really. She's going to bake you a pie."

"But I don't want pie!" Evan wailed. "I don't like it here, Mum! She hurt me. She squeezed my shoulder so hard—"

"Evan, I'm sure she didn't mean to. She's just trying to joke with you. She wants you to like her. Give her a chance—okay?"

Evan started to protest, but thought better of it.

"I'm relying on you," his mother went on, turning her eyes to the kitchen. They could both see Kathryn at the worktop, her broad back to them, hacking away at something with the big kitchen knife.

"But she's . . . weird!" Evan protested.

"Listen, Evan, I understand how you're feeling," his mother said. "But you won't have to spend all your time with her. There are a lot of kids in this neighbourhood. Take Trigger for a walk. I'll bet you'll make some friends your age. She's an old woman, Evan. She won't want you hanging round all the time."

"I suppose so," Evan muttered.

His mother bent down suddenly and gave him a hug, pressing her cheek against his. The hug, he knew, was supposed to cheer him up. But it only made him feel worse.

"I'm relying on you," his mother repeated in his ear.

Evan decided to try and be braver about this. "I'll help you carry the suitcase up to my room," he said.

They carried it up the narrow staircase. His room was actually a study. The walls were lined with bookshelves filled with old hardback books. A large mahogany desk stood in the centre of the room. A narrow bed had been made up under the single, curtained window.

The window faced out onto the back garden, a long green rectangle with the pebble-dashed garage to the left, a tall picket fence to the right.

A small, fenced-in area stretched across the back of the garden. It looked like some sort of dog run.

The room smelled musty. The sharp aroma of mothballs invaded Evan's nose.

Trigger sneezed. He rolled onto his back, his legs racing in the air.

Trigger can't stand this place either, Evan thought. But he kept his thought to himself, smiling bravely at his mother, who quickly unpacked his suitcase, nervously checking her watch.

"I'm late. Don't want to miss my plane," she said. She gave him another hug, longer this time. Then she took a ten-dollar note from her purse and stuffed it into his shirt pocket. "Buy yourself a treat. Be good. I'll hurry back as fast as I can."

"Okay. Bye," he said, his chest feeling fluttery, his throat as dry as cotton. The smell of her perfume momentarily drowned out the mothballs.

He didn't want her to leave. He had such a bad feeling.

You're just scared, he scolded himself.

"I'll phone you from Atlanta," she shouted as she disappeared down the stairs to say goodbye to Kathryn.

Her perfume disappeared.

The mothballs returned.

Trigger uttered a low, sad howl, as if he knew

what was happening, as if he knew they were being abandoned here in this strange house with the strange old woman.

Evan picked Trigger up and nose-kissed his cold, black nose. Putting the dog back down on the worn carpet, he made his way to the window.

He stood there for a long while, one hand holding the curtains aside, staring down at the small, green garden, trying to calm the fluttering in his chest. After a few minutes, he heard his mother's car back down the gravel drive. Then he heard it roll away.

When he could no longer hear it, he sighed and plopped down on the bed. "It's just you and me now, Trigger," he said glumly.

Trigger was busily sniffing behind the door.

Evan stared up at the walls of old books.

What am I going to do here all day? he asked himself, propping his head in his hands. No Nintendo. No computer. He hadn't seen a TV in his great-aunt's small living room. What am I going to do?

Sighing again, he picked himself up and walked along the bookshelves, his eyes scanning the titles. There were lots of science books and textbooks, he saw. Books on biology and astronomy, ancient Egypt, chemistry texts, and medical books. Several shelves were filled with dusty, yellowed books. Maybe Kathryn's husband, Evan's great-uncle, had been some sort of scientist.

Nothing here for me to read, he thought glumly.

He pulled open the cupboard door.

"Oh!"

He cried out as something leapt out at him.

"Help! Please—help!"

Everything went black.

"Help! I can't see!" Evan screamed.

Evan staggered back in fear as the warm blackness crept over him.

It took him a few seconds to realize what it was. His heart still thudding in his chest, he reached up and pulled the screeching black cat off his face.

The cat dropped silently to the ground and padded to the doorway. Evan turned and saw Kathryn standing there, an amused grin on her face.

How long had she been standing there? he wondered.

"Sarabeth, how did you get in there?" she asked in a playfully scolding tone, bending down to speak to the cat. "You must have given the boy a fright."

The cat mewed and rubbed against Kathryn's bare leg.

"Did Sarabeth scare you?" Kathryn asked Evan, still smiling. "That cat has a strange

17

sense of humour. She's evil. Pure evil." She chuckled as if she'd said something funny.

"I'm okay," Evan said uncertainly.

"Watch out for Sarabeth. She's evil," Kathryn repeated, bending down and picking the cat up by the scruff of the neck, holding her up in the air in front of her. "Evil, evil, evil."

Seeing the cat suspended in the air, Trigger uttered an unhappy howl. His stubby tail went into motion, and he leapt up at the cat, barking and yipping, missed, and leapt again, snapping at Sarabeth's tail.

"Down, Trigger! Get down!" Evan cried.

Struggling to get out of Kathryn's arms, the cat swiped a clawed black paw at her, screeching in anger and fear. Trigger barked and howled as Evan struggled to pull the excited cocker spaniel away.

Evan grabbed hold of Trigger as the cat swung to the floor and disappeared out of the door. "Bad dog. Bad dog," Evan whispered. But he didn't really mean it. He was glad Trigger had scared the cat away.

He looked up to see Kathryn still filling the doorway, staring down at him sternly. "Bring the dog," she said in a low voice, her eyes narrowed, her pale lips pursed tightly.

"Huh?" Evan gripped Trigger in a tight hug.

"Bring the dog," Kathryn repeated coldly. "We can't have animals fighting in this house."

18

"But Aunt Kathryn—" Evan started to plead, then remembered she couldn't hear him.

"Sarabeth is a bad one," Kathryn said, not softening her expression. "We can't get her riled, can we?" She turned and started down the stairs. "Bring the dog, Evan."

Holding Trigger tightly by the shoulders with both hands, Evan hesitated.

"I have to take care of the dog," Kathryn said sternly. "Come."

Evan was suddenly filled with dread. What did she mean, *take care* of the dog?

A picture flashed into his mind of Kathryn standing at the doorway with the bloody kitchen knife in her hand.

"Bring the dog," Kathryn insisted.

Evan gasped. What was she going to *do* to Trigger?

"I will take care of you, doggie," Kathryn repeated, frowning at Trigger. The dog whimpered in reply.

"Come, Evan. Follow me," she said impatiently.

Seeing that he had no choice, Evan obediently carried Trigger down the stairs and followed his aunt to the back garden. "I'm prepared," she said, turning to make sure he was following.

Despite her age—she was at least eighty—she walked with long, steady strides. "I knew you were bringing a dog, so I made sure I was prepared."

Trigger licked Evan's hand as they walked across the garden to the long, fenced-in area at the back. "It's a special place for your dog," Kathryn said, reaching up to grab one end of the rope that stretched across the run. "Attach this to the collar, Evan. Your dog will have fun here." She frowned disapprovingly at

20

Trigger. "And there will be no problems with Sarabeth."

Evan felt very relieved that this was all Kathryn wanted to do to Trigger. But he didn't want to leave Trigger tied up in this prison in the back of the garden. Trigger was a house dog. He wouldn't be happy by himself out here.

But Evan knew he had no way of arguing with his aunt. Kathryn is clever in a way, he thought bitterly as he hooked Trigger's collar to the rope. Since she won't learn sign language and won't lip-read, it means she gets to do whatever she wants, and no one can tell her no.

He bent down and gave Trigger's warm head a pat and looked up at the old woman. She had her arms crossed in front of her chest, her blue eyes glowing brightly in the sunlight, a cold smile of triumph on her face.

"That's a good boy," she said, waiting for Evan to get up before starting back to the house. "I knew when I looked at you. Come to the house, Evan. I have cookies and milk. You'll enjoy them." Her words were kind, but her voice was hard and cold.

Trigger sent up an unhappy howl as Evan followed Kathryn to the house. Evan turned, intending to go back and comfort the dog. But Kathryn grabbed his hand in an iron grip, and, staring straight ahead, led him to the kitchen door.

The kitchen was small and cluttered and very warm. Kathryn motioned for him to sit at a small table against the wall. The table was covered with a plastic, checked tablecloth. She frowned, her eyes studying him, as she brought over his snack.

He downed the oatmeal raisin cookies and milk, listening to Trigger howl in the back garden. Oatmeal raisin wasn't his favourite, but he was surprised to find that he was hungry. As he gobbled them down, Kathryn stood at the doorway, staring intently at him, a stern expression on her face.

"I'm going to take Trigger for a walk," he announced, wiping the milk moustache off his upper lip with the paper napkin she had given him.

Kathryn shrugged and wrinkled up her face.

Oh. Right. She can't hear me, Evan thought. Standing at the kitchen window, he pointed to Trigger, then made a walking motion with two fingers. Kathryn nodded.

Whew, he thought. This is going to be hard.

He waved goodbye and hurried to free Trigger from his prison in the back garden.

A few minutes later, Trigger was tugging at the leash, sniffing the flowers along the kerb as Evan made his way up the street. The other houses on the street were about the same size as Kathryn's, he saw. And they all had small, neatly trimmed, square front gardens.

He saw some little kids chasing each other around a birch tree. And he saw a middle-aged man in bright orange swimming trunks washing his car with a garden hose in his drive. But he didn't see any kids of his age.

Trigger barked at a squirrel and tugged the leash out of Evan's hand. "Hey—come back!" Evan called. Trigger, disobedient as always, took off after the squirrel.

The squirrel wisely climbed a tree. But Trigger, his eyesight not what it once had been, continued the chase.

Running at full speed, calling the dog's name, Evan followed him around a corner and halfway down the block before Trigger finally realized he had lost the race.

Breathing hard, Evan grabbed the leash handle. "Gotcha," he said. He gave the leash a tug, trying to lead the panting dog back to Kathryn's street.

Trigger, sniffing around a dark tree trunk, pulled the other way. Evan was about to pick up the stubborn dog when he was startled by a hand grabbing his shoulder.

"Hey—who are *you*?" a voice demanded.

Evan spun round to find a girl standing behind him, staring at him with dark brown eyes. "Why'd you grab my shoulder like that?" he asked, his heart still pounding.

"To scare you," she said simply.

"Yeah. Well..." Evan shrugged. Trigger gave a hard tug at the leash and nearly pulled him over.

The girl laughed.

She was pretty, he thought. She had short, wavy brown hair, almost black, and flashing brown eyes, and a playful, teasing smile. She was wearing an oversized yellow T-shirt over black lycra leggings, and bright yellow Nikes.

"So who *are* you?" she demanded again.

She certainly wasn't the shy type, he decided. "I'm me," he said, letting Trigger lead him round the tree.

"Have you moved into the Winterhalter

house?" she asked, following him.

He shook his head. "No. I'm just visiting."

She frowned in disappointment.

"For a couple of weeks," Evan added. "I'm staying with my aunt. Actually, she's my great-aunt."

"What's so great about her?" the girl cracked.

"Nothing," Evan replied without laughing. "That's for sure."

Trigger sniffed at a beetle on a fat brown leaf.

"Is that your bike?" Evan asked, pointing to the red BMX bike lying on the grass behind her.

"Yeah," she replied.

"It's cool," he said. "I've got one like it."

"I like your dog," she said, eyeing Trigger. "He looks really stupid. I like stupid dogs."

"Me, too. I suppose." Evan laughed.

"What's his name? Does he have a stupid name?" She bent down and tried to pat Trigger's back, but he moved away.

"His name's Trigger," Evan said, and waited for her reaction.

"Yeah. That's pretty stupid," she said thoughtfully. "Especially for a cocker spaniel."

"Thanks," Evan said uncertainly.

Trigger turned to sniff the girl's hands, his tail wagging furiously, his tongue hanging down to the ground.

"I've got a stupid name, too," the girl admitted. She waited for Evan to ask.

"What is it?" he said finally.

"Andrea," she said.

"That's not a stupid name."

"I hate it," she said, pulling a blade of grass off her leggings. "Annndreeea." She stretched the name out in a deep, cultured voice. "It sounds so stuck up, as if I should be wearing a corduroy pinafore dress with a prim, white blouse, walking a toy poodle. So I make everyone call me Andy."

"Hi, Andy," Evan said, patting Trigger. "My name is—"

"Don't tell me!" she interrupted, clamping a hot hand over his mouth.

She certainly *isn't* shy, he thought.

"Let me guess," she said. "Is it a stupid name, too?"

"Yeah," he nodded. "It's Evan. Evan Stupid."

She laughed. "That's a *really* stupid name."

He felt glad that he'd made her laugh. She was cheering him up, he realized. A lot of the girls back home didn't appreciate his sense of humour. They thought he was silly.

"What are you doing?" she asked.

"Walking Trigger. You know. Exploring the neighbourhood."

"It's pretty boring," she said. "Just a lot of houses. Want to go into town? It's only a few streets away." She pointed down the street.

Evan hesitated. He hadn't told his aunt he was going into town. But, what the heck, he thought. She wouldn't care.

Besides, what could possibly happen?

"Okay," Evan said. "Let's explore the town."

"I have to go to a toy shop and look for a present for my cousin," Andy said, hoisting her bike up by the handlebars.

"How old are you?" Evan asked, tugging Trigger towards the street.

"Twelve."

"Me, too," he said. "Can I have a go on your bike?"

She shook her head as she climbed onto the narrow seat. "No, but I'll let you run alongside." She laughed.

"You're a riot," he said sarcastically, hurrying to keep up as she began to pedal.

"And you're stupid," she called back play-fully.

"Hey, *Annnndreeeea*—wait for me!" he called, stretching the name out to annoy her.

A few blocks later, the houses ended and they entered the town centre, a three-block stretch of low two-storey shops and offices. Evan saw a small brick post office, a barbers with an old-fashioned barber's pole outside, a grocers, a drive-in bank, and a hardware shop with a large sign in the window proclaiming a sale on birdseed.

"The toy shop is in the next street," Andy said, walking her bike along the pavement. Evan tugged Trigger's leash, encouraging him to keep up the pace. "Actually there are two toy shops, an old one and a new one. I like the old one best."

"Let's check it out," Evan said, examining the cluttered window display of the video shop on the corner.

I wonder if Aunt Kathryn has a video, he thought. He quickly dismissed the idea. No way. . . .

The toy shop was in an old timber building that hadn't been painted in years. A small hand-painted sign in the dust-smeared window proclaimed: WAGNER'S NOVELTIES & SUNDRIES. There were no toys on display.

Andy leaned her bike against the front of the building. "Sometimes the owner can be a little grumpy. I don't know if he'll let you bring your dog in."

"Well, let's give it a try," Evan said, pulling open the door. Tugging hard on his leash, Trigger led the way into the shop.

Evan found himself in a dark, low-ceilinged,

29

narrow room. It took a while for his eyes to adjust to the dim light.

Wagner's looked more like a warehouse than a shop. There were floor-to-ceiling shelves against both walls, jammed with boxes of toys, and a long display counter that ran through the centre of the shop, leaving narrow aisles that even someone as skinny as Evan had to squeeze through.

At the front of the shop, slumped on a tall stool behind an old-fashioned wooden cash register sat a grumpy-looking man with a single tuft of white hair in the centre of a red, bald head. He had a drooping white moustache that seemed to frown at Evan and Andy as they entered.

"Hi," Andy said timidly, giving the man a wave.

He grunted in reply and turned back to the newspaper he was reading.

Trigger sniffed the low shelves excitedly. Evan looked around at the stacks of toys. It appeared from the thick layer of dust that they'd been sitting there for a hundred years. Everything seemed tossed together, dolls next to building sets, art materials mixed in with old action figures that Evan didn't even recognize, a toy drum kit underneath a pile of footballs.

He and Andy were the only customers in the shop.

"Do they have Nintendo games?" Evan asked

her, whispering, afraid to break the still silence.

"I don't think so," Andy whispered back. "I'll ask." She shouted up to the front, "Do you have Nintendo games?"

It took a while for the man to answer. He scratched his ear. "Don't stock them," he grunted finally, sounding annoyed by the interruption.

Andy and Evan wandered towards the back of the shop. "Why do you like this place?" Evan whispered, picking up an old cap pistol with a cowboy holster.

"I just think it's cool," Andy replied. "You can find some real treasures here. It's not like other toy shops."

"That's for sure," Evan said sarcastically. "Hey—look!" He picked up a lunchbox with a cowboy dressed in black emblazoned on its side. "Hopalong Cassidy," he read. "Who's Hopalong Cassidy?"

"A cowboy with a stupid name," Andy said, taking the old lunchbox from him and examining it. "Look—it's made of metal, not plastic. Wonder if my cousin would like it. He likes stupid names, too."

"It's a pretty weird present," Evan said.

"He's a pretty weird cousin," Andy cracked. "Hey, look at this." She put down the old lunchbox and picked up an enormous box. "It's a magic set. 'Astound your friends. Perform one

31

hundred amazing tricks'," she read.

"That's a lot of amazing tricks," Evan said.

He wandered farther back into the dimly lit shop, Trigger leading the way, sniffing furiously. "Hey—" To Evan's surprise, a narrow doorway led into a small back room.

This room, Evan saw, was even darker and dustier. Stepping inside, he saw worn-looking stuffed animals tossed into crates, games in faded, yellowed boxes, baseball gloves with the leather worn thin and cracked.

Who would want this junk? he thought.

He was about to leave when something caught his eye. It was a blue tin, about the size of a tin of soup. He picked it up, surprised by how heavy it was.

Bringing it close to his face to examine it in the dim light, he read the faded label: MONSTER BLOOD. Below that, in smaller type, it read: SURPRISING MIRACLE SUBSTANCE.

Hey, this looks cool, he thought, turning the can around in his hand.

He suddenly remembered the ten dollars his mother had stuffed into his shirt pocket.

He turned to see the shop owner standing in the doorway, his dark eyes wide with anger. "What are you *doing* out here?" he bellowed.

Trigger yipped loudly, startled by the man's booming voice.

Evan gripped the leash, pulled Trigger close. "Uh...how much is this?" he asked, holding up the tin of Monster Blood.

"Not for sale," the owner said, lowering his voice, his moustache seeming to frown unpleasantly with the rest of his face.

"Huh? It was on the shelf here," Evan said, pointing.

"It's too old," the man insisted. "Probably no good any more."

"Well, I'll take it, anyway,"—Evan said. "Can I have it for less since it's so old?"

"What is it?" Andy asked, appearing in the doorway.

"I don't know," Evan told her. "It looks cool. It's called Monster Blood."

"It's not for sale," the man insisted.

Andy pushed past him and took the tin from

Evan's hand. "Ooh, I want one, too," she said, turning the tin around in her hand.

"There's only one," Evan told her.

"You sure?" She began searching the shelves.

"It's no good, I'm telling you," the owner insisted, sounding exasperated.

"I need one, too," Andy said to Evan.

"Sorry," Evan replied, taking the tin back. "I saw it first."

"I'll buy it from you," Andy said.

"Why don't you two *share* it?" the owner suggested.

"You mean you'll sell it to us?" Evan asked eagerly.

The man shrugged and scratched his ear.

"How much?" Evan asked.

"You sure you don't have another one?" Andy demanded, going back to the shelf, pushing a pile of stuffed pandas out of her way. "Or maybe two? I could keep one and give one to my cousin."

"Two dollars, I suppose," the man told Evan. "But I'm telling you, it's no good. It's too old."

"I don't care," Evan said, reaching into his shirt pocket for the ten-dollar note.

"Well, don't bring it back to me complaining," the man said grumpily, and headed towards the cash register at the front of the shop.

A few minutes later, Evan walked out into the bright daylight carrying the blue tin.

Trigger panted excitedly, wagging his stubby tail, pleased to be out of the dark, dusty shop. Andy followed them out, an unhappy expression on her face.

"Didn't you buy the lunchbox?" Evan asked.

"Don't change the subject," she snapped. "I'll give you five dollars for it." She reached for the tin of Monster Blood.

"No way," Evan replied. He laughed. "You really like to get your own way, don't you!"

"I'm an only child," she said. "What can I tell you? I'm spoiled."

"Me, too," Evan said.

"I have an idea," Andy said, pulling her bike off the shop front wall. "Let's share it."

"Share it?" Evan said, shaking his head. "Oh, yeah. I'll share it the way you shared your bike."

"You want to ride the bike home? Here." She shoved it at him.

"No way," he said, pushing it back towards her. "I wouldn't ride your stupid bike now. It's a girl's bike anyway."

"It is not," she insisted. "Why is it a girl's bike?"

Evan ignored the question and, pulling at Trigger's leash to keep the old dog moving, started walking back towards his aunt's house.

"Why is it a girl's bike?" Andy repeated, walking the bike beside him.

"Tell you what," Evan said. "Let's go back to

my aunt's house and open up the tin. I'll let you play with it for a while."

"Wow," Andy said sarcastically. "You're a great guy, Evan."

"I know," he said, grinning.

Kathryn was sitting in the big armchair in the living room when Evan and Andy arrived. Who is she talking to? he wondered, hearing her voice. She seemed to be arguing excitedly with someone.

Leading Andy into the room, Evan saw that it was just Sarabeth, the black cat. As Evan entered, the cat turned and walked haughtily out of the room.

Kathryn stared at Evan and Andy, a look of surprise on her face. "This is Andy," Evan said, gesturing to his new friend.

"What have you got there?" Kathryn asked, ignoring Andy and reaching out a large hand for the blue tin of Monster Blood.

Evan reluctantly handed it to her. Frowning, she rolled it around in her hand, stopping to read the label, moving her lips as she read. She held the tin for ages, seeming to study it carefully, then finally handed it back to Evan.

As Evan took it back and started to go up to his room with Andy, he heard Kathryn say something to him in a low whisper. He couldn't quite hear what she'd said. It sounded like, "Be careful." But he couldn't be sure.

He turned to see Sarabeth staring at him from the doorway, her yellow eyes glowing in the dim light.

"My aunt is totally deaf," Evan explained to Andy as they climbed the stairs.

"Does that mean you can play your stereo as loud as you want?" Andy asked.

"I don't think Aunt Kathryn has a stereo," Evan said.

"That's too bad," Andy said, walking around Evan's room, pulling back the curtains and looking down on Trigger, huddled unhappily in his pen.

"Is she really your great-aunt?" Andy asked. "She doesn't look very old."

"It's the black hair," Evan replied, putting the tin of Monster Blood on the desk in the centre of the room. "It makes her look young."

"Hey—look at all these old books on magic stuff!" Andy exclaimed. "I wonder why your aunt has all these."

She pulled one of the heavy, old volumes from the shelf and blew away a layer of dust from the top. "Maybe she plans to come up here and cast a spell on you while you're sleeping, and turn you into a newt."

"Maybe," Evan replied, grinning. "What *is* a newt, anyway?"

Andy shrugged. "Some kind of lizard, I think." She flipped through the yellowed pages of the old book. "I thought you said there was nothing to do here," she told Evan. "You could read all these cool books."

"Thrills and chills," Evan said sarcastically.

Replacing the book on the shelf, Andy came over to the desk and stood next to Evan, her eyes on the tin of Monster Blood. "Open it up. It's so old. It's probably all disgusting and rotten."

"I hope so," Evan said. He picked up the tin and studied it. "No instructions."

"Just pull the top off," she said impatiently.

He tugged at it. It wouldn't budge.

"Maybe you need a tin opener or something," she said.

"Very helpful," he muttered, studying the label again. "Look at this. No instructions. No ingredients. Nothing."

"Of course not. It's Monster Blood!" she exclaimed, imitating Count Dracula. She grabbed Evan's neck and pretended to strangle him.

He laughed. "Stop! You're not helping."

He slammed the can down on the desktop— and the lid popped off.

"Hey—look!" he cried.

She let go of his neck, and they both peered inside the can.

The substance inside the tin was bright green. It shimmered like jelly in the light from the overhead lamp.

"Touch it," Andy said.

But before Evan had a chance, she reached a finger in and poked it. "It's cold," she said. "Touch it. It's really cold."

Evan poked it with his finger. It was cold, thicker than jelly, heavier.

He pushed his finger beneath the surface. When he pulled his finger out, it made a loud sucking noise.

"Gross," Andy said.

Evan shrugged. "I've seen worse."

"I bet it glows in the dark," Andy said, hurrying over to the light switch by the door. "It looks like green that glows in the dark."

She turned off the ceiling light, but late afternoon sunlight still poured in through the window. "Try the cupboard," she instructed Evan excitedly.

Evan carried the tin into the cupboard. Andy followed and closed the door. "Yuck. Mothballs," she cried. "I can't breathe."

The Monster Blood definitely glowed in the dark. A circular ray of green light seemed to shine from the tin.

"Wow. That's really cool," Andy said, holding her nose to keep out the pungent aroma of the mothballs.

"I've had other stuff that did this," Evan said, more than a little disappointed. "It was called Alien Stuff or Yucky Glop, something like that."

"Well, if you don't want it, I'll have it," Andy replied.

"I didn't say I didn't want it," Evan said quickly.

"Let's get out of here," Andy begged.

Evan pushed open the door and they rushed out of the cupboard, slamming the door shut behind them. Both of them sucked in fresh air for a few seconds.

"Whew, I hate that smell!" Evan declared. He looked round to see that Andy had taken a handful of Monster Blood from the tin.

She squeezed it into her palm. "It feels even colder outside the tin," she said, grinning at him. "Look. When you squeeze it flat, it pops right back."

"Yeah. It probably bounces, too," Evan said,

unimpressed. "Try bouncing it against the floor. All those things bounce like rubber."

Andy rolled the glob of Monster Blood into a ball and dropped it to the floor. It bounced back up into her hand. She bounced it a little harder. This time it rebounded against the wall and went flying out of the bedroom door.

"It bounces really well," she said, chasing it out into the hall. "Let's see if it stretches." She grabbed it with both hands and pulled, stretching it into a long string. "Yup. It stretches, too."

"Big deal," Evan said. "The stuff I had before bounced and stretched really well, too. I thought this stuff was going to be different."

"It stays cold, even after it's been in your hand," Andy said, returning to the room.

Evan glanced at the wall and noticed a dark, round stain by the floorboard. "Uh-oh. Look, Andy. That stuff stains."

"Let's take it outside and toss it around," she suggested.

"Okay," he agreed. "We'll go out the back. That way, Trigger won't get lonely."

Evan held out the tin, and Andy replaced the ball of Monster Blood. Then they headed downstairs and out to the back garden, where they were greeted by Trigger, who acted as if they'd been away for at least twenty years.

The dog finally calmed down, and sat down in the shade of a tree, panting noisily. "Good boy,"

Evan said softly. "Take it easy. Take it easy, old boy."

Andy reached into the tin and pulled out a green glob. Then Evan did the same. They rolled the stuff in their hands until they had two ball-shaped globs. Then they began to play catch with them.

"It's amazing how they don't lose their shape," Andy said, tossing a green ball high in the air."

Evan shielded his eyes from the late afternoon sun and caught the ball with one hand. "All this stuff is the same," he said. "It isn't so great."

"Well, I think it's cool," Andy said defensively.

Evan's next toss was too high. The green ball of gunk sailed over Andy's outstretched hands.

"Whoa!" Andy cried.

"Sorry," Evan called.

They both stared as the ball bounced once, twice, then landed right in front of Trigger.

Startled, the dog jumped to his feet and lowered his nose to sniff it.

"No, boy!" Evan called. "Leave it alone. Leave it alone, boy!"

As disobedient as ever, Trigger lowered his head and licked the glowing green ball.

"No, boy! Drop! Drop!" Evan called, alarmed.

He and Andy both lunged towards the dog.

But they were too late.

Trigger picked up the ball of Monster Blood in his teeth and began chewing it.

"No, Trigger!" Evan shouted. "Don't swallow it. Don't swallow!"

Trigger swallowed it.

"Oh, no!" Andy cried, balling her hands into fists at her sides. "Now there isn't enough left for us to share!"

But that wasn't what was troubling Evan. He bent down and prised apart the dog's jaws. The green blob was gone. Swallowed.

"Stupid dog," Evan said softly, releasing the dog's mouth.

He shook his head as troubling thoughts poured into his mind.

What if the stuff makes Trigger sick? Evan wondered.

What if the stuff is poison?

"Are we going to make that pie today?" Evan asked his aunt, writing the question on a pad of lined yellow paper he had found on the desk in his room.

Kathryn read the question while adjusting her black ponytail. Her face was as white as cake flour in the morning sunlight filtering through the kitchen window.

"Pie? What pie?" she replied coldly.

Evan's mouth dropped open. He decided not to remind her.

"Go and play with your friends," Kathryn said, still coldly, patting Sarabeth's head as the black cat walked past the breakfast table. "Why do you want to stay inside with an old witch?"

It was three days later. Evan had tried to be friendly to his aunt. But the more he tried, the colder she had become.

She's horrible. She's really horrible, he

thought, as he ate the last spoonful of cereal from his bowl of shredded wheat. That was the only cereal she had. Evan struggled to get it down every morning. Even with milk, the cereal was so dry and she wouldn't even let him put sugar on it.

"Looks as if it might rain," Kathryn said, and took a long sip of the strong tea she had brewed. Her teeth clicked noisily as she drank.

Evan turned his eyes to the bright sunlight outside the window. What made her think it was going to rain?

He glanced back at her, sitting opposite him at the small kitchen table. For the first time, he noticed the pendant around her neck. It was cream-coloured and sort of bone-shaped.

It *is* a bone, Evan decided.

He stared hard at it, trying to decide if it was a real bone, from some animal maybe, or a bone carved out of ivory. Catching his stare, Kathryn reached up with a large hand and tucked the pendant inside her blouse.

"Go and see your girlfriend. She's a pretty one," Kathryn said. She took another long sip of tea, again clicking her teeth as she swallowed.

Yes. I've *got* to get out of here, Evan thought. He pushed his chair back, stood up, and carried his bowl to the sink.

I can't take much more of this, Evan thought miserably. She hates me. She really does.

He hurried up the stairs to his room, where he brushed his curly red hair. Staring into the mirror, he thought of the phone call he had received from his mother the night before.

She had phoned just after dinner, and he could tell immediately from her voice that things weren't going well down in Atlanta.

"How's it going, Mum?" he had asked, so happy to hear her voice, even though she was nearly a thousand miles away.

"Slowly," his mother had replied hesitantly.

"What do you mean? How's Dad? Did you find a house?" The questions seemed to pour out of him like air escaping a balloon.

"Whoa. Slow down," Mrs Ross had replied. She sounded tired. "We're both fine, but it's taking a little longer to find a house than we thought. We just haven't found anything we like."

"Does that mean—" Evan started.

"We found one really nice house, very big, very pretty," his mother interrupted. "But the school you'd go to isn't very good."

"Oh, that's okay. I don't have to go to school," Evan joked.

He could hear his father saying something in the background. His mother covered the receiver to reply.

"When are you coming to pick me up?" Evan asked eagerly.

It took his mother a while to answer. "Well . . .
that's the problem," she said finally. "We may
need a few more days down here than we
thought. How's it going up there, Evan? Are you
okay?"

Hearing the bad news that he'd have to stay
even longer with Kathryn had made Evan feel
like screaming and kicking the wall. But he
didn't want to upset his mother. He told her he
was fine and that he'd made a new friend.

His father had taken the phone and offered a
few encouraging words. "Hang in here," he had
said just before ending the conversation.

I'm hanging in, Evan had thought glumly.

But hearing his parents' voices had made him
even more homesick.

Now it was the next morning. Putting down
his hairbrush, he examined himself quickly in
his dresser mirror. He was wearing denim cut-
offs and a red Gap T-shirt.

Downstairs, he hurried through the kitchen,
where Kathryn appeared to be arguing with
Sarabeth, ran out of the back door, then jogged
to the back garden to get Trigger. "Hey,
Trigger!"

But the dog was asleep, lying on his side in the
centre of his run, gently snoring.

"Don't you want to go to Andy's house?" Evan
asked quietly.

Trigger stirred, but didn't open his eyes.

"Okay. See you later," Evan said. He made sure Trigger's water bowl was filled, then headed to the front of the house.

He was halfway down the next block, walking slowly, thinking about his parents so far away in Atlanta, when a boy's voice called, "Hey—you!" And two boys stepped onto the pavement in front of him, blocking his way.

Startled, Evan stared from one boy to the other. They were twins. Identical twins. Both were big, beefy boys, with short, white-blond hair and round, red faces. They were both wearing dark T-shirts with the names of heavy-metal bands on the front, baggy shorts, and high-top trainers, untied, without socks. Evan guessed they were about fourteen or fifteen.

"Who are *you*?" one of them asked menacingly, narrowing his pale grey eyes, trying to act tough. Both twins moved closer, forcing Evan to take a big step back.

These two are twice my size, Evan realized, feeling a wave of fear sweep over him.

Are they just acting tough? Or do they really mean to give me trouble?

"I—I'm staying with my aunt," he stammered, shoving his hands into his pockets and taking another step back.

The twins flashed each other quick grins. "You can't walk on this block," one of them said, hovering over Evan.

"Yeah. You're not a resident," the other added.

"That's a big word," Evan cracked, then immediately wished he hadn't said it.

Why can't I ever keep my big mouth shut? he asked himself. His eyes surveyed the neighbourhood, searching for someone who might come to his aid in case the twins decided to get rough.

But there was no one in sight. Front doors were closed. Gardens were empty. Way down the block, he could see a postman, heading the other way, too far away to shout to.

No one around. No one to help him.

And the two boys, their faces set, their eyes still menacing, began to move in on him.

"Where do you think you're going?" one of the twins asked. His hands were balled into fists at his sides. He stepped closer until he was only a few centimetres away from Evan, forcing Evan to take a few steps back.

"To see a friend," Evan replied uncertainly. Maybe they were just bluffing.

"Not allowed," the boy said quickly, grinning at his brother.

They both sniggered and moved towards Evan, forcing him to back off the kerb onto the street.

"You're not a resident," the other one repeated. He narrowed his eyes, trying to look tough.

"Hey, give me a break," Evan said. He tried moving to the side, walking on the street, to get around them. But they both moved quickly to keep him from getting away.

"Maybe you could pay a toll," one of them said.

"Yeah," the other one chimed in quickly. "You could pay the non-resident toll. You know, to get temporary permission for walking on this street."

"I don't have any money," Evan said, feeling his fear grow.

He suddenly remembered he had eight dollars in his pocket. Were they going to mug him? Would they beat him up and *then* mug him?

"You have to pay the toll," one of them said, leering at him. "Let's just see what you've got."

They both moved quickly forward, making a grab for him.

He backed away. His legs suddenly felt heavy with fear.

Suddenly a voice cried out from down the pavement. "Hey—what's going on?"

Evan raised his eyes past the two hulking boys to see Andy speeding towards them on her bike along the kerb. "Evan—hi!" she called.

The twins turned away from Evan to greet the new arrival. "Hi, Andy," one of them said in a mocking tone.

"How's it going, Andy?" the other one asked, imitating his brother.

Andy braked her bike and dropped both feet to the ground. She was wearing bright pink shorts and a yellow sleeveless undershirt top. Her face was red, her forehead beaded with perspiration from cycling so hard.

51

"You two," she said, and made an unpleasant face. "Rick and Tony." She turned to Evan. "Were they bothering you?"

"Well . . ." Evan started hesitantly.

"We were welcoming him to the neighbourhood," the one named Rick said, grinning at his brother.

Tony started to add something, but Andy interrupted. "Well, leave him alone."

"Are you his *mother*?" Tony asked, sniggering. He turned to Evan and made goo-goo baby noises.

"We'll leave him alone," Rick said, stepping towards Andy. "We'll borrow your bike and leave him alone."

"No way," Andy said heatedly.

But before Andy could move, Rick grabbed the handlebars. "Let go!" Andy cried, trying to pull the bike from his grasp.

Rick held tight. Tony shoved Andy hard.

She lost her balance and fell, and the bike toppled over on top of her.

"Ohhh."

Andy uttered a low cry as she hit her head on the concrete kerb. She lay sprawled on the kerb, her hands flailing, the bike on top of her.

Before she could get up, Tony reached down and grabbed the bike away. He swung his legs over the seat and began to pedal furiously. "Wait for me!" his brother called, laughing as he ran alongside him.

In seconds, the twins had disappeared around the corner with Andy's bike.

"Andy—are you okay?" Evan cried, hurrying to the kerb. "Are you okay?"

He grabbed Andy's hand and pulled her to her feet. She stood up groggily, rubbing the back of her head. "I hate those creeps," she said. She brushed the dirt and grass off her shorts and legs. "Ow. That hurt."

"Who *are* they?" Evan asked.

"The Beymer twins," she answered, making a disgusted face. "Real heavy-duty dudes," she added sarcastically. She checked her leg to see if it was cut. It was just scraped. "They think they're so cool, but they're total creeps."

"What about your bike? Should we call the police or something?" Evan asked.

"No need," she said quietly, brushing back her dark hair. "I'll get it back. They've done this before. They'll leave it somewhere when they've finished with it."

"But shouldn't we—" Evan started.

"They just run wild," Andy interrupted. "There's no one at home to check up on them. They live with their grandmother, but she's never around. Did they give you a hard time?"

Evan nodded. "I was afraid I was going to have to pound them," he joked.

Andy didn't laugh. "I'd like to pound them," she said angrily. "Just once. I'd like to pay them back. They pick on all the kids in the neighbourhood. They think they can do whatever they want because they're so big, and because there are two of them."

"Your knee is cut," Evan said, pointing.

"I'd better go home and clean it up," she replied, rolling her eyes disgustedly. "See you later, okay? I have to go somewhere this afternoon, but maybe we can do something tomorrow."

She headed back to her house, rubbing the back of her head.

Evan returned to Kathryn's, walking slowly, thinking about the Beymer twins, daydreaming about fighting them, imagining himself beating them to a pulp in a fight as Andy watched, cheering him on.

Kathryn was dusting the front room as Evan entered. She didn't look up. He headed quickly up the stairs to his room.

Now what am I going to do? he wondered, pacing back and forth. The blue container of Monster Blood caught his eye. He walked over to the bookshelf and picked up the tin from the middle shelf.

He pulled off the lid. The tin was nearly full.

I suppose Trigger didn't eat *that* much, he thought, feeling a little relieved.

Trigger!

He'd forgotten all about him. The poor dog must be hungry.

Putting down the Monster Blood, Evan bombed down the stairs, leaning against the banister and taking the stairs three at a time. Then, running full-out, he practically flew to the dog run at the back of the garden.

"Trigger! Hey—Trigger!" he called.

Halfway across the back garden, Evan could see that something was wrong.

Trigger's eyes were bulging. His mouth was wide open, his tongue flailing rapidly from side to side, white spittle running down his chin hair onto the ground.

"Trigger!"

The dog was gasping hoarsely, each breath a desperate, difficult struggle.

He's choking! Evan realized.

As Evan reached the dog run, Trigger's eyes rolled back, and the dog's legs collapsed under him, his stomach still heaving, the air filled with his loud, hideous gasps.

"Trigger—no!"

Evan dived to his knees beside the dog and began to tug at Trigger's collar. The collar, Evan saw, had become far too tight.

The dog's chest heaved. Thick white spittle flowed from his open mouth.

"Hold on, boy. Hold on!" Evan cried.

The dog's eyes rolled wildly in his head. He didn't seem to see or hear Evan.

"Hold on, fella! Just *hold on*!"

The collar wouldn't budge. It was buried tightly under the dog's fur.

His hands shaking, Evan struggled to pull the collar over Trigger's head.

Come loose, come loose, come *loose*, he begged.

Yes!

Trigger uttered a pained whimper as Evan finally managed to pull the collar away.

"Trigger—it's off! Are you okay?"

Still panting hard, the dog jumped immediately to his feet. He licked Evan's face appreciatively, covering Evan's cheek with his thick saliva, whimpering as if he understood that Evan had just saved his life.

"Easy, boy! Easy, fella!" Evan repeated, but the dog continued to lick him gratefully.

Evan hugged the excited dog. This had been a close call, he knew. If he hadn't come along just then . . .

Well, he didn't want to think about it.

When Trigger finally calmed down, Evan examined the collar. "What made this collar shrink like that, boy?" he asked Trigger.

The dog had walked over to the fence and was frantically slurping water from his bowl.

This is plain weird, Evan thought. The collar couldn't have shrunk. It's made of leather. There was no reason for it to shrink.

Then why did it suddenly start choking Trigger?

Evan turned to Trigger, studying him as the dog lapped greedily at the water, breathing hard. He turned and glanced back at Evan for a second, then returned to his frantic water slurping.

He's *bigger*, Evan decided.

He's definitely bigger.

But Trigger was twelve years old, eighty-four in dog years. Older than Aunt Kathryn.

57

Trigger was too old for a late growth spurt.

It must be my eyes, Evan decided, tossing the collar to the ground. This place must be making me see things.

Kathryn was at the kitchen door, calling Evan to lunch. He poured out a bowl of dry food, shouted goodbye to Trigger, who didn't look up from the water dish, and hurried to the house.

The next morning, an overcast morning with an autumn chill in the air, Evan made his way to Andy's house. He found her huddled under a big maple tree in the neighbour's front garden. "What's going on?" he called.

Then he saw that she was leaning over something, her hands working quickly. "Come and help me!" she cried, not looking up.

Evan came jogging over. "Whoa!" he cried out when he saw that Andy was struggling to free a tortoiseshell cat that had been tied to the tree trunk.

The cat screeched and swiped its paw at Andy. Andy dodged the claws and continued to pull at the big knots in the rope.

"The Beymer twins did this. I know it," she said loudly, over the shrilly protesting cat. "This poor cat has probably been tied up here all night."

The cat, in a panic, shrieked with amazingly human-sounding cries.

"Stay still, cat," Evan said as the terrified cat swiped its claws at Andy again. "Can I help?"

"No. I've almost got it," she replied, tugging at the knot. "I'd like to tie Rick and Tony to this tree."

"Poor, frightened cat," Evan said quietly.

"There," Andy said triumphantly, pulling the rope loose.

The cat gave one last cry of protest, its tail standing straight up. Then it darted away, running at full speed, and disappeared under a tall hedge without looking back.

"Not very polite," Evan muttered.

Andy stood up and sighed. She was wearing faded denim jeans and a pale green, baggy T-shirt that nearly came down to her knees. She lifted the bottom of the shirt to examine a hole the cat had managed to snag in it.

"I can't believe those two creeps," she said, shaking her head.

"Maybe we should call the police or the RSPCA or something," Evan suggested.

"The twins would just deny it," Andy said glumly, shaking her head. Then she added, "And the cat's not a very good witness."

They both laughed.

Evan led the way back to his aunt's house. All the way back, they talked about how they'd like to teach the Beymer twins a lesson. But neither of them had any good ideas.

They found Kathryn concentrating on a jigsaw puzzle at the dining room table.

She looked up when they entered, squinting at them. "You like jigsaw puzzles? I like to keep my mind active, you know. That's why I like puzzles. Your mind can get flabby when you get to be my age. A hundred and twelve."

She slapped the table gleefully at her own wit. Evan and Andy both flashed her agreeable smiles. Then she returned to her puzzle without waiting for a reply.

"She's going to drive me bananas!" Evan exclaimed.

"Evan—she'll hear you!" Andy protested, cupping a hand over his mouth.

"I told you, she's completely deaf. She can't hear me. She doesn't *want* to hear anyone. She *hates* everyone."

"I think she's quite sweet," Andy said. "Why does she wear a bone around her neck?"

"Probably thinks it's cool," Evan cracked.

"Let's go upstairs," Andy urged, pushing him towards the stairs. "I still feel weird talking about your aunt right in front of her."

"You're a crazy old coot," Evan called to Kathryn, a big smile on his face.

Kathryn looked up from her puzzle to cast a cold stare his way.

"She heard you!" Andy cried, horrified.

"Don't be stupid," Evan said, and started

up the stairs, nearly tripping over Sarabeth.

Up in Evan's room, Andy paced uncomfortably. "What do you want to do?"

"Well . . . we could read some of these great books," Evan said sarcastically, pointing to the dusty old books that lined the walls. "Maybe find a spell to cast on the Beymer twins. You know. Turn them into newts."

"Forget about newts," Andy said dryly. "Hey—where's the Monster Blood?" Before Evan could answer, she spotted it on one of the shelves.

They raced across the room for it. Andy got there first and grabbed the tin. "Evan—look," she said, her eyes growing wide with suprise. "What's going on?"

She held up the tin. The green gunk had pushed up the lid and was flowing up out of the tin.

"Huh? Has the lid broken or something?" Evan asked.

He took the tin from her and examined it. Sure enough, the lid had popped off. The gooey green substance was pushing up out of the can.

Evan pulled out a handful of the green gunk. "Weird," he exclaimed. "It's expanding," he said, squeezing it in his hand. "It's definitely growing."

"I suppose so!" Andy exclaimed. "It grew right out of the tin!"

"Hey—it's not cold any more," Evan said. He rolled it into a ball and tossed it to Andy.

"It's really warm," she agreed. "Weird!"

She tried to toss it back to him, but it stuck to her palm. "It's getting sticky," she reported. "Are you sure this is the same stuff?"

"Of course," Evan replied.

"But it wasn't sticky before, remember?" she said.

He pulled another warm hunk of it from the tin. "I suppose it just changes after the can has been opened."

He squeezed the stuff into another ball shape and tossed it to the floor. "Look—it stuck to the floor. It didn't bounce."

"Weird!" Andy repeated.

"Maybe I should throw it in the dustbin," Evan said, prising the sticky glob from the floor. "I mean, what good is it if it doesn't bounce?"

"Hey—no way," Andy said. "We've got to see what it does next."

A soft mewing sound made them both turn towards the door.

Evan was surprised to see Sarabeth standing there, her head cocked, her yellow eyes staring at him.

Or was she staring at the glob of Monster Blood in his hand?

"That cat looks so intelligent," Andy said.

"It's as stupid as every other cat," Evan muttered. "Look. She wants to play ball with the Monster Blood."

"Sorry, cat," Andy said. "It doesn't bounce."

As if she understood, Sarabeth mewed unhappily, turned, and padded silently from the room.

"Now where am I going to keep this stuff?" Evan asked. "It's too big for its tin."

"Here. How about this?" Andy asked. She

reached down to a low shelf and came up with an empty coffee jar.

"Yeah. Okay." Evan tossed his hunk into the coffee jar.

Andy squeezed hers into a flat pancake. "Look. It isn't glowing the way it used to, either," she said, holding the pancake up for Evan to see. "But it's really warm. Almost hot."

"It's *alive*!" Evan screamed playfully. "Run for your life! It's *alive*!"

Andy laughed and began to chase Evan, menacing him with the flat, green pancake. "Come and get your Monster Blood! Come and get it!"

He dodged away, then grabbed it from her hand. He squeezed it together, balling it up in one hand, then tossed it into the coffee jar.

They both peered into the jar. The green substance filled it up a little more than halfway.

"Go ahead. Taste it," Andy urged, poking the jar in his face. "I dare you."

"Huh? No way. I double-dare you," Evan said, pushing the coffee jar back to her.

"Double-darers have to go first," Andy insisted, grinning. "Go ahead. Taste it."

Evan made a disgusted face and shook his head. Then he grabbed a big hunk of it and heaved it at Andy. Laughing, she picked it up off the carpet and tossed it at his face. She threw high, and the green glob stuck to the wall.

Evan reached for another hunk.

They had a messy, hilarious Monster Blood battle till dinnertime. Then, as they tried to clean up, they both heard Trigger through the open window. He was barking loudly out in his pen.

Evan reached the window first. The sky was still grey and overcast. Trigger was leaning on the wooden fence, standing on his hind legs, barking his head off.

"Whoa, Trigger," Evan called. "Calm down!"

"Hey—what's the matter with Trigger?" Andy asked. "Is your dog still growing? He looks so big!"

Evan's mouth dropped open and he uttered a silent gasp, realizing that Andy was right.

Trigger had nearly doubled in size.

"Trigger—come back! Come *back!*"

The big dog continued to run, its giant paws thundering against the concrete.

"*Come back!*" Evan screamed, running with long, desperate strides, his heart thudding, his legs aching with each step as he tried to catch up with the galloping dog.

The night was dark and starless. The street glistened as if it had recently rained.

Trigger's paws hit the pavement, each step a loud thunderclap that seemed to echo forever. His giant ears flapped like wings, twin pennants caught on the wind. His big head bobbed up and down, but he didn't look back.

"Trigger! *Trigger!*"

Evan's voice seemed muffled by the gusting wind, pushed back in his face. He tried shouting louder, but no sound came out at all.

He knew he had to stop the dog from running away. He had to catch the dog and then get help.

Trigger was growing so fast, completely out of control. He was already the size of a pony, and getting larger by the minute.

"Trigger! Trigger! Stop, boy!"

Trigger didn't seem to hear him. Evan's voice didn't seem to carry beyond the gusting, swirling wind.

And still Evan ran, his chest pounding, every muscle aching. And as he ran, he suddenly realized there were others running, too.

Two large figures in front of the stampeding dog.

Two large figures Evan recognized as they fled at full speed, trying to get away from the charging animal.

The Beymer twins. Rick and Tony.

Trigger was chasing them, Evan suddenly realized.

The boys turned a corner, onto an even darker street. Trigger followed, bounding after them. Evan continued to run, bringing up the rear of this dark, mysterious chase.

All was silent now, except for the steady, rhythmic thunder of Trigger's enormous padded paws.

Except for the *clapclapclap* of the Beymer twins' trainers as they darted along the glistening pavement.

Except for the gasp of Evan's breathing as he struggled to keep up.

Suddenly, as Evan watched in horror, the dog rose up on his hind legs. He tilted his head to the sky and let out an ear-piercing howl. Not the howl of a dog. A creature howl.

And then Trigger's features began to transform. His forehead burst forward and enlarged. His eyes grew wide and round before sinking under the protruding forehead. Fangs slid from his gaping mouth, and he uttered another howl to the sky, louder and more chilling than the first.

"He's a monster! A monster!" Evan cried.

And woke up.

Woke up from his frightening dream.

And realized he was in bed, in the study, upstairs in Aunt Kathryn's house.

It had all been a dream, a frightening, wild chase of a dream.

A harmless dream. Except that something still wasn't right.

The bed. It felt so uncomfortable. So cramped.

Evan sat up, alert, wide awake now.

And stared down at his giant feet. His giant hands. And realized how tiny the bed seemed beneath him.

Because he was a giant now.

Because he had grown so huge, so monstrously huge.

And when he saw how big he had become, he opened his mouth wide and began to scream.

His screams woke him up.

This time he really woke up.

And realized that, the first time, he had only dreamed that he was awake. Had only dreamed that he had become a giant.

Dreams upon dreams.

Was he really awake now?

He sat up, blinked, rubbed his eyes, struggled to focus.

Dripping with sweat.

His blankets tossed to the floor.

His pyjamas damp, clinging to his prickly skin.

Nothing seemed familiar. It took a while to shake off the dream, to remember where he was. That he was in his room at Aunt Kathryn's. Awake now. His normal size.

Tossed by the wind, the curtains brushed over him, then were noisily sucked out of the window.

Evan sat up and, still feeling shaky, peered out of the window.

Wisps of grey clouds floated over a pale half-moon. Trees tossed and whispered in the cool night wind.

Only a dream.

A frightening dream. A dream on top of a dream.

He could see Trigger sound asleep, curled up on himself, pressed against the fence wall.

Trigger wasn't a monster. But he was definitely bigger, Evan could see that.

Maybe there's something wrong with him. The troubling thought pushed its way into Evan's mind as he stared down at the sleeping dog.

Maybe it's his glands or something.

Maybe he's eating too much. Or maybe . . .

Evan yawned. He realized he was too sleepy to think clearly. Maybe the next morning he'd see if there was a vet in town.

Yawning again, he started to settle back into bed. But something caught his eye.

The coffee jar on the bookshelf. The jar where he had stored the Monster Blood.

"Hey—" he cried aloud.

The green gunk was bubbling, quivering up over the top of the jar.

"Your dog seems to be quite healthy for his age."
Dr Forrest scratched Trigger gently under the
chin. "Look at all the white hairs," he said,
bringing his face down close to the dog's.
"You're a good old dog, aren't you?"

Trigger licked the doctor's hand appreciatively.

Dr Forrest grinned, pushing his black eye-
glasses up on his narrow nose, the ceiling light
reflecting off his shiny forehead. He wiped his
hand on the front of his white lab coat.

Evan and Andy stood opposite Trigger in the
small, brightly lit surgery. They had both been
tense during the long examination the vet had
given the dog. But now, hearing the doctor's
verdict, they had relaxed expressions on their
faces.

"So you think it's just a late growth spurt?"
Evan repeated.

Dr Forrest nodded, returning to his desk in the

corner. "Highly unusual," he said softly, leaning over the desk to write a note on a pad. "Highly unusual. We'll get a lab report in three or four days. It may tell us more. But the dog seems very healthy to me. I really wouldn't be alarmed."

"But do cocker spaniels usually get this big?" Evan asked, leaning down to scratch Trigger under the chin, the leash looped loosely in his hand.

Trigger wanted to leave. He pulled towards the door. Evan stood up and tugged hard at the leash to keep the dog in place. It took all his strength. Trigger was not only bigger; he was much stronger than he had been a few days before.

"No. Not usually," the vet replied. "That's why I took the hormone tests and the blood and glandular samples. Maybe the lab will have an answer for us."

He finished writing and tore the sheet off the pad. "Here," he said, handing the paper to Evan. "I wrote down the name of a good dog food. Put Trigger on this, and see that he cuts down on his between-meal snacks." He chuckled at his own joke.

Evan thanked the doctor and allowed Trigger to pull them out of the office. Andy jogged after them. In the waiting room outside, a tiny Chihuahua cowered behind the sofa, whimpering at the sight of the big cocker spaniel.

"I'm glad to be out of there," Evan exclaimed as they stepped out on to the pavement.

"Trigger got a very good report," Andy said reassuringly, patting Trigger's head. "Hey, look—his head is wider than my hand!"

"He's nearly as big as a sheepdog!" Evan said miserably. "And Dr Forrest says he's perfectly okay."

"Don't exaggerate," Andy scolded. She glanced at her watch. "Oh, no! I don't believe it. Late for my piano lesson. Again! Mum'll *kill* me!"

She waved goodbye, turned, and ran full speed down the pavement, nearly colliding with an elderly couple coming slowly out of the small grocery shop on the corner.

"Let's go, boy," Evan said, thinking about what Dr Forrest had said. Tugging the leash, he headed out of the small, three-block town. Despite the vet's assurances, Evan was still pretty worried about Trigger.

He stopped outside the grocery shop. "Maybe an ice cream will help cheer me up." He tied Trigger's leash to the red fire extinguisher opposite the grocery shop door. "Stay," he instructed.

Trigger, ignoring Evan, struggled to pull free.

"I'll only be a second," Evan said, and hurried into the shop.

There were three or four people in the shop and it took a bit longer than Evan had expected. When he returned to the pavement ten minutes later, he discovered the Beymer twins busily untying Trigger.

"Hey—let go!" he cried angrily.

They both turned towards him, identical grins on their beefy faces. "Look what we found," one of them teased. The other one successfully untied the leash from the fire extinguisher.

"Hand me that," Evan insisted, holding his chocolate ice cream in one hand, reaching for the leash handle with the other.

The Beymer twin held the leash handle out to Evan—then quickly snapped it back out of his reach. "Gotcha!"

The brothers laughed gleefully and slapped each other a high five.

"Stop messing around," Evan insisted. "Hand me the leash."

"Finders, keepers," one of them said. "Isn't that right, Tony?"

"Yeah," Tony replied, grinning. "It's an ugly dog. But it's *our* ugly dog now."

"Get your own dog, wimp," Rick said nastily. He stepped forward and punched the ice cream out of Evan's hand. It landed on the pavement with a *plop*.

The brothers started to laugh, but their laughter was cut short as Trigger suddenly uttered a low, warning growl. Pulling back his lips, he bared his teeth, and his growl became a snarl.

"Hey—" Rick cried, dropping the leash.

With a loud, angry roar, Trigger reared up and pounced on Rick, forcing him to stagger backwards to the kerb.

Tony had already started to run, his trainers pounding the pavement noisily as he headed at full speed past the vet's surgery, past the post office, and kept going.

"Wait for me! Hey, Tony—wait for me!" Rick stumbled, stood up, and took off after his brother.

Evan grabbed for Trigger's leash—and missed.

"Trigger—whoa! Stop!"

The dog took off after the fleeing twins, barking angrily, his enormous paws thudding loudly on the pavement, picking up speed as he closed in on them.

No, Evan thought, finding himself frozen there on the corner in front of the grocery shop.

No. No. No.

This *can't* be happening.

It's my dream.

Is it coming true?

Evan shuddered, remembering the rest of his dream, remembering how he, too, grew until he was twice his size.

Would that part of the dream also come true?

That afternoon, about an hour before dinner-time, Evan phoned Andy. "Can I come over?" he asked. "I have a small problem."

"Sounds like a big problem," Andy said.

"Yeah. Okay. A big problem," Evan snapped impatiently. "I'm not in the mood to kid around, okay?"

"Okay. Sorry," Andy replied quickly. "Any sign of Rick and Tony? They're not your problem, are they?"

"Not at the moment," he told her. "I told you they had gone by the time I caught up with Trigger. Disappeared. Vanished. Trigger was still barking his head off. Somehow I dragged him home and got him in his pen."

"So what's your problem?" she asked.

"I can't tell you. I have to show you," he said. "I'll be right there. Bye."

He hung up the phone and hurried down the stairs, carrying the bucket. Kathryn was in the kitchen, her back to him, chopping away at something with her big butcher's knife. Evan hurried past and darted out of the door.

Andy's house was a modern, redwood ranch style, with a low hedge of evergreens running along the front. Her dad, she said, was a fanatic about the lawn. It was clipped a perfect three centimetres above the ground, smooth as a carpet. A flower garden stretched along the front of the house, tall orange and yellow tiger lilies bobbing in the gentle breeze.

The front door was open. Evan knocked on the screen door.

"What's with the bucket?" was Andy's greeting as she let him in.

"Look," he said, out of breath from running all the way to her house. He held up the aluminium bucket he had taken from his aunt's garage.

"Oh, wow," Andy exclaimed, raising her hands to her face as she stared into it wide-eyed.

"Yeah. Wow," he repeated sarcastically. "The Monster Blood. It's grown again. Look. It's almost filled this big bucket. What are we going to do?"

"What do you mean, *we*?" Andy teased, leading him into the study.

"Not funny," he muttered.

"You didn't want to share it," she insisted.

"I'll share it now," he said eagerly. "In fact...

do you want it? I'll give it to you for a bargain price—free." He held the bucket out to her.

"Huh-uh." Andy shook her head, crossing her arms in front of her chest. "Put it down, will you?" She pointed to the corner behind the red leather sofa. "Put it over there. It's giving me the creeps."

"Giving *you* the creeps!?" Evan cried. "What am I going to do? Every time I turn round, it grows a bit more. It's growing faster than Trigger!"

"Hey!" they both cried at once.

Both had the same thought, the same frightening memory. Both suddenly remembered that Trigger had eaten a ball of the green gunk.

"Do you think . . ." Evan started.

"Maybe . . ." Andy replied, not waiting for him to finish his thought. "Maybe Trigger's growing because he ate the Monster Blood."

"What am I going to *do*?" Evan wailed, pacing the room nervously, his hands shoved into his jeans pockets. "The stuff is getting bigger and bigger, and so is poor Trigger. I'm all alone here. There's no one who can help me. No one."

"What about your aunt?" Andy suggested, staring at the bucket on the floor in the corner. "Maybe Kathryn can think of something—"

"Are you kidding? She can't hear me. She doesn't *want* to hear me. She *hates* me. She just sits at her jigsaw puzzle and argues with that horrible black cat all day."

"Okay. Forget the aunt," Andy said, making a dispirited face.

"Perhaps if you told Dr Forrest—"

"Oh, yeah, sure," Evan snapped. "He'd really believe that Trigger is turning into a giant because I let him eat Monster Blood."

He threw himself down on the sofa. "I'm all alone here, Andy. There's no one to help me. No one I can even talk to about this."

"Except me?"

"Yeah," he said, locking his eyes on hers. "Except you."

She plopped down on the other end of the sofa. "Well, what can I do?" she asked hesitantly.

He jumped up and carried the bucket over. "Take some of this. Let's split it up."

"Huh? Why don't we just chuck it in the dustbin?" she asked, staring down at it. The green gunk was pushing up near the top of the bucket.

"Chuck it? We can't," he said.

"Of course we can. Come on. I'll show you." She reached for the bucket handle, but he shoved it out of her reach.

"What if it outgrows the dustbin?" he asked. "What if it just keeps growing?"

Andy shrugged. "I don't know."

"Also, I *have* to save it," Evan continued excitedly. "If it's really the thing that's causing Trigger to grow, I'll need it as proof. You know. To show the doctors or whatever. So they can cure Trigger."

"Maybe we should call the police," Andy said thoughtfully, tugging at a strand of hair.

"Oh. Yeah," Evan replied, rolling his eyes. "They'll really believe us. Won't they? 'We bought this stuff in a toy shop, officer, and now it's growing bigger and bigger and it's turning my dog into a giant monster.'"

"Okay, okay. You're right," Andy said. "We can't call the police."

"So, are you going to help me?" Evan demanded. "Will you take some of this stuff?"

"I suppose so," she said reluctantly. "But just a little." She climbed to her feet, carefully stepping around the bucket. "I'll be right back."

She left the room, then quickly returned, carrying an empty coffee jar. "Fill 'er up," she said, smiling.

Evan stared at the coffee jar. "That's *all* you're going to take?" he complained. Then he immediately softened his tone. "Okay. Okay. It's a help."

Andy crouched down and dipped the coffee jar into the middle of the bucket. "Hey!" she cried out. Her hands flew up and she tumbled back onto the floor.

81

"What's wrong?" Evan hurried over to her.

"It was pulling the coffee jar in," she said, her features tight with fear and surprise. "Sucking it. Look."

Evan peered into the bucket. The coffee jar had disappeared under the surface. "Huh?"

"I could feel it pulling," Andy said shakily. She regained her perch over the bucket.

"Let's see," Evan said, and plunged both hands into the middle of the Monster Blood.

"Yuck," Andy said. "This is really gross."

"It's pulling. You're right," Evan agreed. "It feels like it's pulling my hands down. Wow. It's so warm. As if it's alive."

"*Don't say that!*" Andy cried with a shudder. "Just get the jar out, okay?"

Evan had to tug hard, but he managed to pull up the coffee jar, filled to the top with the quivering green substance. "Yuck."

"You sure I have to take this?" Andy asked, not reaching for it even though he was holding it out to her.

"Just for a little while," he said. "Till we think of a better plan."

"Maybe we could feed it to the Beymer twins," Andy suggested, finally taking the jar.

"Then we'd have *giant* Beymer twins," Evan joked. "No, thank you."

"Seriously, you'd better watch out for them," Andy warned. "If Trigger scared them away this morning, they'll be looking to get back at you. They really think they're tough, Evan. They can be vicious. They could really hurt you."

"Thanks for trying to cheer me up," Evan said glumly. He was still pulling tiny, clinging clumps of the Monster Blood off his hands and tossing them into the bucket.

"I was watching a video before you came over. The first Indiana Jones movie. Want to watch it?"

Evan shook his head. "No. I'd better go. Aunt Kathryn was busy making dinner when I left. Chopping up some kind of meat. Another great dinner, sitting there in silence, being stared at by Aunt Kathryn and her cat."

"Poor Evan," Andy said, half teasing, half sympathetic.

He picked up the bucket, now only two-thirds full, and let her walk him to the front door. "Call me later, okay?" she asked.

He nodded and stepped outside. She closed the door behind him.

He was halfway to the pavement when the Beymer twins slipped out from behind the evergreen hedge, their hands clenched into red, beefy fists.

The brothers stepped out of the shadows of the hedge. Their short blond hair caught the late afternoon sunlight. They were both grinning gleefully.

Evan stood frozen in place, staring from one to the other.

No one said a word.

One of the Beymers grabbed the bucket from Evan's hand and tossed it to the ground. The bucket landed with a heavy *thud*, and its thick, green contents oozed onto the grass, making disgusting sucking sounds.

"Hey—" Evan cried, breaking the tense silence.

He didn't have a chance to say more.

The other twin punched him hard in the stomach.

Evan felt the pain radiate through his body. The punch took his breath away. He gasped for air.

He didn't see the next punch. It landed on his cheek just below his right eye.

He howled in pain, and his hands flailed the air helplessly.

Both brothers were hitting him now. And then one of them gave Evan's shoulders a hard shove, and he went sprawling onto the cool, damp grass.

The pain swept over him, blanketing him, followed by a wave of nausea. He closed his eyes, gasping noisily, waiting for the sharp ache in his stomach to fade.

The ground seemed to tilt. He reached out and grabbed it, and held on tightly so he wouldn't fall off.

When he finally managed to raise his head, Andy was standing over him, her eyes wide with alarm. "Evan—"

He groaned and, pushing with both hands, tried to sit up. The dizziness, the spinning, tilting grass, forced him to lie back down.

"Have they gone?" he asked, closing his eyes, willing the dizziness away.

"Rick and Tony? I saw them run away," Andy said, kneeling beside him. "Are you okay? Should I get my mum?"

He opened his eyes. "Yeah. No. I don't know."

"What *happened*?" she demanded.

He raised a hand to his cheek. "Ow!" It was already swollen, too painful to touch.

"They beat you up?"

"Either that or I was hit by a lorry," he groaned.

A few minutes later—it seemed like hours—he was back on his feet, breathing normally, rubbing his swollen cheek. "I've never been in a fight before," he told Andy, shaking his head. "Never."

"It doesn't look as if it was much of a fight," she said, her expression still tight with concern.

He started to laugh, but it made his stomach hurt.

"We'll pay them back," Andy said bitterly. "We'll find a way to pay them back. The creeps."

"Oh. Look. The Monster Blood." Evan hurried over to it.

The bucket lay on its side. The green gunk had oozed onto the grass, forming a wide, thick puddle.

"I'll help you get it back in the bucket," Andy said, leaning over to stand the bucket up. "Hope it doesn't ruin the grass. My dad'll have a cow if his precious lawn is hurt!"

"It's so heavy," Evan said, groaning as he tried to push the glob into the bucket. "It doesn't want to move."

"Let's try picking up handfuls," Andy suggested.

"Whoa. It doesn't want to come apart," Evan said in surprise. "Look. It sticks together."

"It's like chewing gum," Andy said. "Ever see them make chewing gum in those toffee machines? The stuff just sticks together in one big glob."

"This isn't toffee," Evan muttered. "It's disgusting."

Working together, they managed to lift the entire green ball and drop it into the bucket. The stuff made a sickening sucking sound as it filled the bucket, and both Evan and Andy had trouble pulling their hands out of it.

"It's so sticky," Andy said, making a disgusted face.

"And warm," Evan added. He finally managed to free his hands from it. "It's as if it's trying to swallow my hands," he said, wiping his hands on his T-shirt. "Sucking them in."

"Take it home," Andy said. She looked up to the house to see her mother motioning to her from the front window. "Uh-oh. Dinnertime. I've got to go." Her eyes stopped at his swollen cheek. "Wait till your aunt sees you."

"She probably won't even notice," Evan said glumly. He picked up the bucket by the handle. "What are we going to do with this stuff?"

"We'll take it back to the toy shop tomorrow," Andy replied, taking long strides across the lawn to the house.

"Huh?"

"That's what we'll do. We'll simply take it back."

Evan didn't think it was such a great idea. But he didn't have the strength to argue about it now. He watched Andy disappear into the house. Then he headed slowly back to Kathryn's, his head throbbing, his stomach aching.

Creeping along the wall of the house, he slipped into the garage through the side door to hide the bucket of Monster Blood. Sliding it behind an overturned wheelbarrow, he realized that the bucket was full to the top.

But I gave Andy a big hunk of it, he thought. The bucket had been only two-thirds full.

I'll have to find a bigger place to put it, he decided. Tonight. Maybe there's a box or something in the basement.

He crept into the house, determined to clean himself up before seeing Aunt Kathryn. She was still busy in the kitchen, he saw, leaning over the cooker, putting the last touches to the dinner. He tiptoed up the stairs and had a wash. Unable to do much about his swollen, red cheek, he changed into a clean pair of baggy shorts and a fresh T-shirt, and carefully brushed his hair.

As they sat down at the dining room table, Kathryn's eyes fell on Evan's swollen cheek. "You been in a fight?" she asked, squinting suspiciously at him. "You're a little roughneck, aren't you? Just like your father. Chicken was always getting into scrapes, always picking on boys twice his size."

"I wasn't exactly picking on them," Evan muttered, spearing a chunk of beef from his stew with his fork.

All through dinner, Kathryn stared at his swollen cheek. But she didn't say another word.

She doesn't care if I'm hurt or not, Evan thought miserably.

She really doesn't care.

She didn't even ask if it hurts.

In a way, he was grateful. He didn't need her getting all upset, making a fuss because he'd been in a fight, maybe calling his parents in Atlanta and telling them.

Well . . . she couldn't call his parents. She couldn't use the phone, since she couldn't hear.

Evan downed his big plate of beef stew. It was pretty good, except for the vegetables.

The silence seemed so *loud*. He began thinking about his problem—the Monster Blood.

Should he tell Kathryn about it?

He could write down the whole problem on the yellow pad and hand it to her to read. It would feel so good to tell someone, to have an adult take over the problem and handle it.

But not his Aunt Kathryn, he decided.

She was too weird.

She wouldn't understand.

She wouldn't know what to do.

And she wouldn't care.

Andy was right. They had to carry the stuff back to the toy shop. Give it back. Just get rid of it.

But in the meantime, he had to find something to keep it in.

Evan waited in his room until he heard Kathryn go to bed, a little after ten o'clock. Then he crept down the stairs and headed out to the garage.

It was a cool, clear night. Crickets sent up a relentless curtain of noise. The black sky glittered with tiny specks of stars.

The round beam of light from the torch in his hand darted across the drive, leading Evan to the dark garage. As he entered, something scuttled across the floor near the back wall.

Maybe it was just a dead leaf, blown by the wind when I opened the door, he thought hopefully.

He moved the torch unsteadily, beaming it onto the overturned wheelbarrow. Then the light darted across the garage ceiling as he bent down, reached behind the wheelbarrow, and pulled out the bucket of Monster Blood.

He moved the light to the centre of the bucket, and gasped.

The green substance was quivering up over the top.

It's growing much faster than before, he thought.

I've *got* to find something bigger to hide it in—just for tonight.

The bucket was too heavy to carry with one hand. Tucking the torch into his armpit, he gripped the bucket handle with both hands and hoisted the bucket off the floor.

Struggling to keep from spilling it, he made his way into the dark house. He paused at the door to the basement steps, silently setting the heavy bucket down on the linoleum floor.

He clicked the light switch on the wall. Somewhere downstairs a dim light flickered on, casting a wash of pale yellow light over the concrete floor.

There's got to be something to put this stuff in down there, Evan thought. Hoisting up the bucket, he made his way slowly, carefully down the steep, dark staircase, leaning his shoulder against the wall to steady himself.

Waiting for his eyes to adjust to the pale light, he saw that the basement was one large room, low-ceilinged and damp. It was cluttered with boxes, stacks of old newspapers and magazines, and old furniture and appliances covered in stained, yellowed bed sheets.

Something brushed his face as he stepped away from the stairs.

He uttered a silent cry and, dropping the

92

bucket, raised his hands to swipe at the thick cobwebs that seemed to reach out for him. They clung to his skin, dry and scratchy, as he frantically pulled at them.

He suddenly realized it wasn't the web that was moving against his cheek.

It was a spider.

With a sharp intake of breath, he brushed it away. But even after he saw the insect scuttle across the floor, he could still feel its prickly feet moving on his face.

Moving quickly away from the wall, his heart pounding now, his eyes searching the open wooden shelves hidden in shadow against the far wall, he stumbled over something on the floor.

"Oh!" He fell headfirst over it, throwing his hands forward to break his fall.

A human body!

Someone lying there under him!

No.

Calm down, Evan. Calm down, he instructed himself.

He pulled himself shakily to his feet.

It was a dressmaker's dummy he had stumbled over. Probably a model of Kathryn when she was younger.

He rolled it out of the way as his eyes searched the shadowy room for a container to store the Monster Blood. What was that long, low

93

object in front of the worktable?

Moving closer, he saw that it was an old bathtub, the insides stained and peeling. It's big enough, he realized, and quickly decided to store the green gunk inside it.

With a loud groan, he hoisted the bucket into the side of the old bath. His stomach muscles were still sore from the punch he had taken, and the pain shot through his body.

He waited for the aching to fade, then tilted the bucket. The thick green substance rolled out of the bucket and hit the bottom of the bath with a sickening soft *plop*.

Evan put the bucket aside and stared down at the Monster Blood, watching it ooze, spreading thickly over the bottom of the bathtub. To his surprise, the tub appeared nearly half full.

How fast was this stuff growing?!

He was leaning over the tub, about to make his way back upstairs, when he heard the cat screech.

Startled, he let go of the side of the tub just as Sarabeth leapt onto his back. Evan didn't have time to cry out as he toppled forward, over the edge of the tub and into the thick, green gunk.

Evan landed hard on his elbows, but the thick Monster Blood softened the fall. He heard the cat screech again and pad away.

He sank into the ooze, his arms and legs flailing, trying to lift himself away. But the sticky substance was sucking him down, pulling him with surprising force.

His whole body seemed to be held by it, stuck as if in cement, and now it was quivering up, bubbling silently, rising up to his face. I'm going to suffocate, he realized.

It's trying to choke me.

The warmth of it spread across his body, invaded his chest, his legs, his throat.

I can't move.

I'm stuck.

It's trying to choke me.

No!

He pulled his head up just as the green gunk began to cover his face.

Then he struggled to twist his body, to twist himself around in it. With great effort, panting loudly, hoarse cries escaping his open lips, he pulled himself up into a sitting position.

The green substance rose up even bigger, as if it were reaching up to him, reaching to drag him back down into it.

Evan gripped the side of the tub with both hands, held on to it tightly, and began to force himself up. Up, up from the clinging, pulling ooze. Up from the strange force that seemed to be drawing him back with renewed power.

Up. Up.

"No!" he managed to scream as the warm, green ooze slid over his shoulders.

"No!"

It was gripping his shoulders now, sliding around his neck, sucking him down, pulling him back into its sticky depths.

Down. Down.

It's got me, he realized.

It's got me now.

"No!" Evan screamed aloud as the green gunk bubbled up to his neck.

Pulling him. Pulling him down.

"No!"

Try again. Up.

Try again.

Up. Up.

Yes!

Gripping the sides of the tub, he was moving upward, pulling himself, hoisting himself, straining with all of his strength.

Yes! Yes! He was beating it.

He was stronger than it was. One more tug and he would be free.

With a relieved sigh, he dropped over the side of the tub onto the cool basement floor.

And lay there, pressed against the damp concrete, waiting to catch his breath.

When he looked up, Sarabeth stood a few metres away, her head cocked to one side, her yellow eyes peering into his, an expression of supreme satisfaction on her dark feline face.

The next morning, after a fitful, restless sleep, Evan brought the pad of yellow lined paper and a marker to the breakfast table.

"Well, well," Kathryn greeted him, placing a bowl of shredded wheat in front of him, "you certainly look like something the cat dragged in!" She laughed, shaking her head.

"Don't mention *cat* to me," Evan muttered. He shoved the bowl of cereal aside and pointed to the pad in his hand.

"Don't let your cereal get soggy," Kathryn scolded, reaching to push the bowl back to him. "You get more of the vitamins that way. And it's good roughage."

"I don't care about your stupid roughage," Evan said moodily, knowing she couldn't hear him. He pointed to the pad again, and then began to write, scribbling quickly in big, black letters.

His writing caught her interest. She moved around the table and stood behind him, her eyes on the pad as he wrote his desperate message.

I HAVE A PROBLEM, he wrote. I NEED YOUR HELP. THE BATHTUB DOWNSTAIRS IS OVER-FLOWING WITH GREEN MONSTER BLOOD AND I CAN'T STOP IT.

He put down the marker and held the pad up close to her face.

Looking up at her from the chair, seeing her pale face in the morning sunlight as she leaned over him in her grey towelling bathrobe, Kathryn suddenly looked very old to him. Only her eyes, those vibrant, blue eyes running quickly over his words, seemed youthful and alive.

Her lips were pursed tightly in concentration as she read what he had written. Then, as Evan stared eagerly up at her, her mouth spread into a wide smile. She tossed back her head and laughed.

Completely bewildered by her reaction, Evan slid his chair back and jumped up. She rested a hand on his shoulder and gave him a playful shove.

"Don't kid an old woman!" she exclaimed, shaking her head. She turned and walked back to her side of the table. "I thought you were serious. I suppose you're not like your father at all. He never played any silly jokes or tricks. Chicken was always such a serious boy."

"*I don't care about Chicken!*" Evan shouted, losing control, and tossed the pad angrily onto the breakfast table.

His aunt burst out laughing. She didn't seem to notice that Evan was glaring at her in frustration, his hands tightened into fists at his sides.

"Monster Blood! What an imagination!" She wiped tears of laughter from her eyes with her fingers. Then suddenly, her expression turned serious. She grabbed his earlobe and squeezed it. "I warned you," she whispered. "I warned you to be careful."

"Ow!"

When he cried out in pain, she let go of his ear, her eyes glowing like blue jewels.

I've got to get out of here, Evan thought, rubbing his tender earlobe. He turned and strode quickly from the kitchen and up to his room.

I knew she wouldn't be any help, he thought bitterly.

She's just a crazy old lady.

I should pull her down to the basement and *show* her the disgusting stuff, he thought, angrily tossing the clothes he had worn yesterday onto the floor.

But what's the point? She'd probably laugh at that, too.

She isn't going to help me.

He had only one person he could rely on, he knew.

Andy.

He called her, dialling her number with trembling fingers.

"Hi. You're right," he said, not giving her a chance to say anything. "We have to take the stuff back to the shop."

"*If* we can carry it," Andy replied, sounding worried. "That hunk of Monster Blood you gave me—it outgrew the coffee jar. I put it in my parents' ice bucket, but it's outgrowing that."

"How about a plastic rubbish bag?" Evan suggested. "You know. One of the really big ones. We can probably carry it in a couple of those."

"It's worth a try," Andy said. "This stuff is so disgusting. It's making all these sick noises, and it's really sticky."

"Tell me about it," Evan replied gloomily, remembering the night before. "I took a *swim* in it."

"Huh? You can explain later," she said impatiently. "The toy shop opens at ten, I think. I can meet you on the corner in twenty minutes."

"Good." Evan hung up the phone and headed to the garage to get a plastic dustbin bag.

Andy turned up with her plastic bag wrapped around the handlebars of her BMX bike. Once again, Evan had to walk along beside her on foot. His plastic bag was bulging, and so heavy he had to drag it over the pavement. He couldn't lift it.

"The bathtub was nearly full to the top," he told Andy, groaning as he struggled to pull the bag over the kerb. "I'm afraid it's going to burst out of this bag."

"Only two blocks to go," she said, trying to sound reassuring. A car rolled by slowly. The driver, a teenager with long black hair, stuck his head out of the window, grinning. "What's in the bag? A dead body?"

"Just rubbish," Evan told him.

"That's for sure," Andy muttered as the car rolled away.

Several people stopped to stare at them as they entered town. "Hi, Mrs Winslow," Andy called to a friend of her mother's.

Mrs Winslow waved, then gave Andy a curious stare, and headed into the grocery shop.

Andy climbed off her bike and walked. Evan continued to drag his bulging bag behind him.

They made their way to the next block, then started to cross the street to the toy shop.

But they both stopped short in the middle of the street.

And gaped in shock.

The door and window of the shop were boarded up. A small, hand-printed sign nailed to the top of the door read: OUT OF BUSINESS.

Desperate to get rid of the disgusting contents of the rubbish bags, Evan pounded on the door anyway.

"Come on—somebody! Somebody, open up!"

No reply.

He pounded with both fists.

Silence.

Finally, Andy had to pull him away.

"The shop is closed," a young woman called from across the street. "It closed down a few days ago. See? It's all boarded up and everything."

"Very helpful," Evan muttered under his breath. He slammed his hand angrily against the door.

"Evan—stop. You'll hurt yourself," Andy warned.

"Now what?" Evan demanded. "Got any more fantastic ideas, Andy?"

She shrugged. "It's your turn to come up with something brilliant."

Evan sighed miserably. "Maybe I could give it to Kathryn and tell her it's beef. Then she'd chop it up with that knife she's always carrying around."

"I don't think you're thinking too clearly at the moment," Andy said, putting a sympathetic hand on his shoulder.

They both stared down at the rubbish bags. They appeared to be moving—expanding and contracting, as if the green globs inside were *breathing*!

"Let's go back to Kathryn's," Evan said, his voice trembling. "Maybe we'll think of something on the way."

Somehow they managed to drag the Monster Blood back to Kathryn's house. The sun was now high up in the sky. As they headed for the back garden, Evan was drenched with sweat. His arms ached. His head throbbed.

"Now what?" he asked weakly, letting go of the bulging rubbish bag.

Andy leaned her bike against the side of the garage. She pointed to the big aluminium dustbin next to the garage door. "How about that? It looks pretty sturdy." She walked over to it to investigate. "And look—the lid clamps down."

"Okay," Evan agreed, wiping his forehead with the sleeve of his T-shirt.

Andy pulled off the lid of the dustbin. Then she dumped in the contents of her bag. It hit the

104

bottom with a sick, squishy sound. Then she hurried to help Evan.

"It's so heavy," Evan groaned, struggling to pull the bag up.

"We can do it," Andy insisted.

Working together, they managed to slide the Monster Blood from the plastic bag. It rolled out like a tidal wave, sloshing noisily against the sides of the can, rising up as if trying to escape.

With a loud sigh of relief, Evan slammed the metal lid down on top of it and clamped the handles down.

"Whoa!" Andy cried.

They both stared at the can for a long moment, as if expecting it to explode or burst apart. "Now what?" Evan asked, his features tight with fear.

Before Andy could reply, they saw Kathryn step out of the kitchen door. Her eyes searched the back garden until she spotted them. "Evan— good news!" she called.

Glancing back at the dustbin, Evan and Andy came hurrying over. Kathryn was holding a yellow piece of paper in her hand. A telegram.

"Your mother is coming to pick you up this afternoon," Kathryn said, a wide smile on her face.

I think Kathryn is glad to get rid of me, was Evan's first thought.

And then, dismissing that thought, he leapt

up and whooped for joy. It was the best news he'd ever received.

"I'm outta here!" he exclaimed after his aunt had returned to the house. "I'm outta here! I can't wait!"

Andy didn't appear to share his joy. "You're leaving your aunt a nice little surprise over there," she said, pointing to the dustbin.

"I don't care! I'm outta here!" Evan repeated, raising his hand for Andy to slap him a high five.

She didn't cooperate. "Don't you think we have to tell someone about the Monster Blood? Or do something about it—before you leave?"

But Evan was too excited to think about that now. "Hey, Trigger!" he called, running to the dog's pen at the back of the garden. "Trigger— we're going home, boy!"

Evan pulled open the gate—and gasped.

"Trigger!"

The dog that came bounding towards him *looked* like Trigger. But the cocker spaniel was the size of a pony! He had *doubled* in size since the day before!

"No!" Evan had to hit the dirt as Trigger excitedly tried to jump on him. "Hey—wait!"

Before Evan could get up, Trigger began barking ferociously. The huge dog was already past the gate and thundering across the back garden towards the street.

"I don't believe it!" Andy cried, raising her hands to her face, staring in shock as the enormous creature bounded around the side of the house and out of sight. "He's so—big!"

"We've got to stop him! He might hurt someone!" Evan cried.

"Trigger! Trigger—come back!" Still off balance, Evan started to run, calling frantically. But he stumbled over Andy's bike and fell onto the dustbin.

"No!" Andy shrieked, looking on helplessly as the metal bin toppled over, with Evan sprawled on top of it. The bin hit the drive with a loud *clang*.

The lid popped off and rolled away.

The green gunk poured out.

It oozed away from the bin, then stopped and appeared to stand up. Quivering, making loud sucking sounds, it righted itself, pulling itself up tall.

As the two kids stared in silent horror, the quivering green mass appeared to come to life, like a newly born creature pulling itself up, stretching, looking around.

Then, with a loud sucking sound, it arched towards Evan, who was still sprawled on the toppled bin.

"Get up, Evan!" Andy cried. "Get up! It's going to roll right over you!"

"Noooooo!"

Evan uttered an animal cry, a sound he had never made before—and rolled away as the quivering green ball bounced towards him.

"Run, Evan!" Andy screamed. She grabbed his hand and pulled him to his feet. "It's alive!" she cried. "Run!"

The Monster Blood heaved itself against the garage wall. It seemed to stick there for a brief second. Then it peeled off, and came bouncing towards them with surprising speed.

"Help! Help!"

"Somebody—please—*help*!"

Screaming at the top of their lungs, Evan and Andy took off. Scrambling as fast as he could, his legs weak and rubbery from fear, Evan followed Andy down the drive towards the front garden.

"Help! Oh, please! Help us!"

Evan's voice was hoarse from screaming. His

109

heart thudded in his chest. His temples throbbed.

He turned and saw that the Monster Blood was right behind them, picking up speed as it bounced across the garden, making disgusting squishing noises with each bounce.

Plop. Plop. Plop.

A robin, pulling at a worm in the grass, didn't look up in time. The trembling green mass rolled over it.

"Oh!" Evan moaned, turning back to see the bird sucked into the green ball. Its wings flapping frantically, the bird uttered a final cry, then disappeared inside.

Plop. Plop. Plop.

The Monster Blood changed direction, still bouncing and quivering, and leaving white stains on the grass like enormous, round footsteps.

"It's alive!" Andy screamed, her hands pressed against her cheeks. "Oh, my God—it's *alive!*"

"What can we do? What can we do?" Evan didn't recognize his own terrified voice.

"It's catching up!" Andy screamed, pulling him by the hand. "Run!"

Gasping loudly, they made their way to the front of the house.

"Hey—what's happening?" a voice called.

"Huh?"

Startled by the voice, Evan stopped short. He looked over to the pavement to see the Beymer twins, matching grins on their beefy faces.

"My favourite punch bag," one of them said to Evan. He raised his fist menacingly.

They took a few steps towards Evan and Andy. Then their grins faded and their mouths dropped open in horror as the gigantic green mass appeared, heading down the drive, rolling as fast as a bicycle.

"Look out!" Evan screamed.

"Run!" Andy cried.

But the two brothers were too startled to move.

Their eyes bulging with fear, they threw their hands up as if trying to shield themselves.

Plop. Plop. Plop.

The enormous ball of Monster Blood picked up speed as it bounced forward. Evan shut his eyes as it hit the twins with a deafening *smack*.

"Ow!"

"No!"

Both brothers cried out, flailing their arms, struggling to pull themselves free.

"Help us! Please—help us!"

Their bodies twisted and writhed as they struggled.

But they were stuck tight. The green gunk oozed over them, covering them completely.

Then it pulled them inside with a loud sucking *pop*.

Andy shielded her eyes. "Sick," she muttered. "Oooh. Sick."

Evan gasped in helpless horror as the Beymer brothers finally stopped struggling.

Their arms went limp. Their faces disappeared into the quivering gunk.

The sucking sounds grew louder as the two boys were pulled deeper and deeper inside. Then the Monster Blood bounced high, turned, and started back up the drive.

Andy and Evan froze, unsure of which way to head.

"Split up!" Evan cried. "It can't go after us both!"

Andy returned his frightened stare. She opened her mouth, but no sound came out.

"Split up! Split up!" Evan repeated shrilly.

"But—" Andy started.

Before she could say anything, the front door of the house burst open, and Kathryn stepped out onto the front step.

"Hey—what are you kids doing? What's *that*?" she cried, gripping the screen door, her eyes filling with horror.

Picking up speed, the giant ball bounded towards the step.

Kathryn threw up her hands in fright. She stood frozen for a long moment, as if trying to make sense of what she was seeing. Then, leaving the front door wide open, she spun round and fled into the house.

Plop. Plop.

The Monster Blood hesitated at the front porch.

It bounced in place once, twice, three times, as if considering what to do next.

Evan and Andy gaped in horror from across the lawn, trying to catch their breath.

A wave of nausea swept over Evan as he saw the Beymer twins, still visible deep within the quivering glob, faceless prisoners bouncing inside it.

Then suddenly, the Monster Blood bounced high and hurtled up the stairs of the porch.

"No!" Evan screamed as it squeezed through the open doorway and disappeared into the house.

From the middle of the garden, Andy and Evan heard Kathryn's bloodcurdling scream.

"It's got Aunt Kathryn," Evan said weakly.

Evan reached the house first. He had run so fast, his lungs felt as if they were about to burst.

"What are you going to do?" Andy called, following close behind.

"I don't know," Evan replied. He grabbed on to the screen door and propelled himself into the house.

"Aunt Kathryn!" Evan screamed, bursting into the living room.

The enormous glob filled the centre of the small room. The Beymer twins were outlined in its side as it bounced and quivered, oozing over the carpet, leaving its sticky footprints in its path.

It took Evan a few seconds to see his aunt. The bouncing hunk of Monster Blood had backed her against the fireplace.

"Aunt Kathryn—run!" Evan cried.

But even he could see that she had nowhere to run.

"Get out of here, kids!" Kathryn cried, her voice shrill and trembling, suddenly sounding very old.

"But, Aunt Kathryn—"

"Get out of here—now!" the old woman insisted, her black hair wild about her head, her eyes, those blue, penetrating eyes, staring hard at the green glob as if willing it away.

Evan turned to Andy, uncertain of what to do.

Andy's hands tugged at the sides of her hair, her eyes wide with growing fear as the seething green glob made its way steadily closer to Evan's aunt.

"Get out!" Kathryn repeated shrilly. "Save your lives! I made this thing! Now I must die for it!"

Evan gasped.

Had he heard correctly?

What had his aunt just said?

The words repeated in his mind, clear now, so clear—and so frightening.

"I made this thing. Now I must die for it."

"No!"

Gaping in horror, as the sickening glob of Monster Blood pushed towards his aunt, Evan felt the room tilt and begin to spin. He gripped the back of Kathryn's armchair as pictures flooded his mind.

He saw the strange bone pendant Kathryn always wore around her neck.

The mysterious books that lined the walls of his bedroom.

Sarabeth, the black cat with the glowing yellow eyes.

The black shawl Kathryn always wrapped around her shoulders in the evening.

"I made this thing. Now I must die for it."

Evan saw it all now, and it began to come clear to him.

Evan remembered the day he and Andy had brought home the tin of Monster Blood from the toy shop. Kathryn had insisted on seeing it.

On studying it.

On touching it.

He remembered the way she had rolled the tin around in her hands, examining it so carefully. Moving her lips silently as she read the label.

What had she been doing? What had she been saying?

A thought flashed into Evan's mind.

Had she been casting a spell on the can?

A spell to make the Monster Blood grow? A spell to terrify Evan?

But why? She didn't even know Evan.

Why did she want to frighten him? To ... *kill* him?

"Be careful," she had called to him after handing the blue tin back. "Be careful."

It was a real warning.

A warning against her spell.

"You did this!" Evan shouted in a voice he didn't recognize. The words burst out of him. He had no control over them.

"You did this! You cast a spell!" he repeated, pointing an accusing finger at his aunt.

He saw her blue eyes shimmer as they read his lips. Then her eyes filled with tears, tears that overflowed onto her pale cheeks.

"No!" she cried. "No!"

"You did something to the tin! You did this, Aunt Kathryn!"

"No!" she cried, shouting over the sickening grunts and *plops* of the mountainous ball that nearly hid her from view.

"No!" Kathryn cried, her back pressed tightly against the mantelpiece. "I didn't do it! *She* did!"

And she pointed an accusing finger at Andy.

Andy?

Was Aunt Kathryn accusing *Andy*?

Evan spun round to confront Andy.

But Andy turned, too.

And Evan realized immediately that his aunt wasn't pointing at Andy. She was pointing past Andy to Sarabeth.

Standing in the doorway to the living room, the black cat hissed and arched her back, her yellow eyes flaring at Kathryn.

"She did it! She's the one!" Kathryn declared, pointing frantically.

The enormous glob of green Monster Blood bounced back, retreated a step, as if stung by Kathryn's words. Shadows shifted inside the glob as it quivered, catching the light filtering in through the living room window.

Evan stared at the cat, then turned his eyes to Andy. She shrugged, her face frozen in horror and bewilderment.

Aunt Kathryn is crazy, Evan thought sadly.

She's totally lost it.

She isn't making any sense.

None of this makes sense.

"She's the one!" Kathryn repeated.

The cat hissed in response.

The glob bounced in place, carrying the motionless Beymer brothers inside.

"Oh—look!" Evan cried to Andy as the black cat suddenly rose up on its hind legs.

Andy gasped and squeezed Evan's arm. Her hand was as cold as ice.

Still hissing, the cat grew like a shadow against the wall. It raised its claws, swiping the air. Its eyes closed, and it became consumed in darkness.

No one moved.

The only sounds Evan could hear were the bubbling of the green glob and the pounding of his own heart.

All eyes were on the cat as it rose up, stretched, and grew. And as it grew, it changed its shape.

Became human.

With shadowy arms and legs in the eerie darkness.

And then the shadow stepped away from the darkness.

And Sarabeth was now a young woman with fiery red hair and pale skin and yellow eyes, the same yellow cat eyes that had haunted Evan since he'd arrived. The young woman was dressed in a swirling black gown down to her ankles.

She stood blocking the doorway, staring accusingly at Kathryn.

"You see? She's the one," Kathryn said, quietly now. And the next words were intended only for Sarabeth: "Your spell over me is broken. I will do no more work for you."

Sarabeth tossed her red hair behind a black-cloaked shoulder and laughed. "I'll decide what you will do, Kathryn."

"No," Kathryn insisted. "For twenty years, you have used me, Sarabeth. For twenty years you have imprisoned me here, held me in your spell. But now I will use this Monster Blood to escape."

Sarabeth laughed again. "There is no escape, fool. All of you must die now. *All* of you."

"All of you must die," Sarabeth repeated. Her smile revealed that she enjoyed saying those words.

Kathryn turned to Evan, her eyes reflecting her fear. "Twenty years ago, I thought she was my friend. I was all alone here. I thought I could trust her. But she cast a spell on me. And then another. Her dark magic made me deaf. She refused to let me lip-read or learn to sign. That was one way she kept me her prisoner."

"But, Aunt Kathryn—" Evan started.

She raised a finger to her lips to silence him.

"Sarabeth forced me to cast the spell on the tin of Monster Blood. She had warned me that I was allowed no guests, you see. I was her slave. Her personal servant for all these years. She wanted me all to herself, to do her evil bidding.

"When you arrived," Kathryn continued, her back still pressed against the fireplace, "she first decided to scare you away. But that was impossible. You had nowhere to go. Then she became desperate to get you out of the way. She was terrified that you would learn her secret, that you would somehow free me of her spell. So Sarabeth decided that you had to die."

Kathryn's eyes fell. She sighed. "I'm so sorry, Evan. I had no choice, no will of my own." She turned her eyes to Sarabeth. "But no more. No more. No more. As I plunge myself into this ghastly creation, Sarabeth, I will end your spell. I will end your hold over me."

"The children will still die," Sarabeth said quietly, coldly.

"What?" Kathryn's eyes filled with fury. "I will be gone, Sarabeth. You can let the children go. You have no reason to do them harm."

"They know too much," Sarabeth replied softly, crossing her slender arms in front of her, her yellow eyes aglow.

"We've got to get out of here," Evan whispered to Andy, staring at the seething green glob.

"But how?" Andy whispered back. "Sarabeth is blocking the doorway."

Evan's eyes darted around the small room, searching for an escape route.

Nothing.

Sarabeth raised one hand and drew it towards her slowly, as if summoning the green glob.

It quivered once, twice, then moved obediently in the direction of her hand.

"No! Sarabeth—stop!" Kathryn pleaded.

Ignoring Kathryn, Sarabeth gestured with her hand again.

The green gunk bubbled and rolled forward.

"Kill the children," Sarabeth commanded.

The enormous glob picked up speed as it rolled across the carpet towards Evan and Andy.

"Let's rush the door," Evan suggested to Andy, as they backed away from the rolling Monster Blood.

"She'll never let us past," Andy cried.

"Kill the children!" Sarabeth repeated, raising both hands high above her head.

"Maybe one of us can get by her!" Evan cried.

"It's too late!" Andy shrieked.

The bouncing, pulsating, green glob was just a few metres away.

"We—we're going to be sucked in!" Evan screamed.

"Kill the children!" Sarabeth screamed triumphantly.

The glob rolled forward.

Evan sighed, feeling all hope sink. Frozen in place, he felt as if he weighed a tonne.

Andy grabbed his hand.

They both closed their eyes and held their breath, and waited for the impact.

To their surprise, the Monster Blood emitted a deafening roar.

"Huh?"

Evan opened his eyes. Andy, he saw, was staring at the doorway, beyond Sarabeth.

The Monster Blood hadn't roared.

"Trigger!" Evan cried.

The huge dog bounded into the doorway, its deafening bark echoing off the low ceiling.

Sarabeth tried to get out of the dog's way. But she was too late.

Thrilled to see Evan, Trigger enthusiastically leapt at Sarabeth—and pushed her from behind.

Under the weight of the gigantic paws,

Sarabeth staggered forward . . . forward . . . forward—raising her hands as she collided with the Monster Blood.

There was a wet *smack* as Sarabeth hit the surface of the green glob.

Then loud, disgusting sucking noises.

Her hands hit first. They disappeared quickly. And then Sarabeth was in up to her elbows.

And then the glob seemed to give a hard tug, and her body hit the surface. Then her face was pulled in, covered over.

Sarabeth never uttered a sound as she was pulled inside.

Whimpering with joy, completely unaware of what he had done, the dog loped into the room and headed for Evan.

"Down, boy! Down!" Evan cried, as Trigger happily leapt at him.

And as the dog jumped, he began to shrink.

"Trigger!" Evan called in astonishment, reaching out to hold the dog.

Trigger didn't seem to notice that he was changing. He licked Evan's face as Evan held on tightly.

In seconds, Trigger was back to normal cocker spaniel size.

"Look—the glob is shrinking, too!" Andy cried, squeezing Evan's shoulder.

Evan turned to see that the green glob was rapidly growing smaller.

As it shrunk, the Beymer brothers fell to the floor.

They didn't move. They lay facedown in a crumpled heap. Their open eyes stared lifelessly. They didn't appear to be breathing.

Then one blinked. The other blinked.

Their mouths opened and closed.

"Ohhh." One of them uttered a long, low groan.

Then, pulling themselves up slowly, they both looked around the room, dazed.

The trapped robin had also fallen to the floor. Chirping furiously, it flapped its wings wildly and fluttered about the room in a panic—until it found the open living room window and sailed out.

Andy held on to Evan as they stared at the Monster Blood, expecting Sarabeth to reappear, too.

But Sarabeth was gone.

Vanished.

The Monster Blood, shrunk to its original size, lay lifeless, inert, a dull green spot on the carpet, no bigger than a tennis ball.

The Beymer brothers stood up uncertainly, their eyes still reflecting terror and confusion. They stretched as if testing their arms and legs, seeing if their muscles still worked. Then they scrambled out of the house, slamming the screen door behind them.

"It's over," Kathryn said softly, moving forward to put an arm around Evan and Andy.

"Sarabeth has gone," Evan said, holding Trigger tightly in his arms, still staring at the tiny wedge of Monster Blood on the floor.

"And I can hear!" Kathryn said jubilantly, hugging them both. "Sarabeth *and* her spells have gone for good."

But as she said this, the screen door swung open and a shadowy figure stepped into the living room doorway.

"Mum!" Evan cried.

He put Trigger down and hurried to greet her, throwing his arms around her in a tight hug.

"What on earth is going on here?" Mrs Ross asked. "Why did those two boys come bursting out like that? They looked scared to *death*!"

"It—it's a little hard to explain," Evan told her. "I'm so glad to see you!"

Trigger was glad, too. When he'd finally finished jumping up and down and whimpering, Kathryn led Evan's mum to the kitchen. "I'll make some tea," she said. "I have a rather long story to tell you."

"I hope it isn't *too* long," Mrs Ross said, glancing back questioningly at Evan. "We have a four o'clock plane to catch."

"Mum, I think you'll find this story interesting," Evan said, flashing Andy an amused look.

The two women disappeared into the kitchen.

Andy and Evan dropped down wearily onto the sofa.

"I suppose you're going forever," Andy said. "I mean, to Atlanta and everything—"

"I'd like to ... uh ... write to you," Evan said, suddenly feeling awkward.

"Yeah. Good," Andy replied, brightening. "And my dad has a phone credit card. Maybe I could get the number and ... you know ... call you."

"Yeah. Great," Evan said.

"Could I ask one small favour?" Andy asked.

"Yeah. Sure," Evan replied, curious.

"Well, it's going to sound strange," Andy said reluctantly. "But can I ... uh ... can I have the little bit of Monster Blood that's left? You know. Sort of as a memento or something?"

"Of course. Okay with me," Evan said.

They both turned their eyes to where it had come to rest on the carpet.

"Hey—" Andy cried in surprise.

It had gone.

Add *more*

to your collection . . .
A chilling preview of
what's next from
R.L. STINE

LET'S GET INVISIBLE!

I found myself in a small, windowless room. The
only light came from the pale yellow ceiling light
behind us in the centre of the attic.

"Push the door all the way open so the light
can get in," I instructed Erin. "I can't see a thing
in here."

Erin pushed open the door and slid a box over
to hold it in place. The she and April crept in to
join Lefty and me.

"It's too big to be a cupboard," Erin said, her
voice sounding even squeakier than usual. "So
what is it?"

"Just a room, I suppose," I said, still waiting
for my eyes to adjust to the dim light.

I took another step into the room. And as I did
so, a dark figure stepped towards me.

I screamed and jumped back.

The other person jumped back, too.

"It's a mirror, dork!" Lefty said, and started to
laugh.

Instantly, all four of us were laughing. Nervous, high-pitched laughter.

It *was* a mirror in front of us. In the pale yellow light filtering into the small, square room, I could see it clearly now.

It was a big, rectangular mirror, about two feet taller than me, with a dark wooden frame. It rested on a wooden base.

I moved closer to it and my reflection moved once again to greet me. To my surprise, the reflection was clear. No dust on the glass, despite the fact that no one had been in here in ages.

I stepped in front of it and started to check out my hair.

I mean, that's what mirrors are for, right?

"Who would put a mirror in a room all by itself?" Erin asked. I could see her dark reflection in the mirror, a few feet behind me.

"Maybe it's a valuable piece of furniture or something," I said, reaching into my jeans pocket for my comb. "You know. An antique."

"Did your parents put it up here?" Erin asked.

"I don't know," I replied. "Maybe it belonged to my grandparents. I just don't know." I ran the comb through my hair a few times.

"Can we go now? This isn't too thrilling," April said. She was still lingering reluctantly in the doorway.

"Maybe it was a carvinal mirror," Lefty said,

pushing me out of the way and making faces into the mirror, bringing his face just inches from the glass. "You know. One of those fun house mirrors that makes your body look like it's shaped like an egg."

"You're already shaped like an egg," I joked, pushing him aside. "At least, your head is."

"You're a *rotten* egg," he snapped back. "You stink."

I peered into the mirror. I looked perfectly normal, not distorted at all. "Hey, April, come in," I urged. "You're blocking most of the light."

"Can't we just leave?" she asked, whining. Reluctantly, she moved from the doorway, taking a few small steps into the room. "Who cares about an old mirror, anyway?"

"Hey, look," I said, pointing. I had spotted a light attached to the top of the mirror. It was oval-shaped, made of brass or some other kind of metal. The bulb was long and narrow, almost like a fluorescent bulb, only shorter.

I gazed up at it, trying to make it out in the dim light. "How do you turn it on, I wonder."

"There's a chain," Erin said, coming up beside me.

Sure enough, a slender chain descended from the right side of the lamp, hanging down about a foot from the top of the mirror.

"Wonder if it works," I said.

"The bulb's probably dead," Lefty remarked.

Good old Lefty. Always an optimist.

"Only one way to find out," I said. Standing on tiptoes, I stretched my hand up to the chain.

"Be careful," April warned.

"Huh? It's just a light," I told her.

Famous last words.

I reached up. Missed. Tried again. I grabbed the chain on the second try and pulled.

The light came on with a startlingly bright flash. Then it dimmed down to normal light. Very white light that reflected brightly in the mirror.

"Hey—that's better!" I exclaimed. "It lights up the whole room. Pretty bright, huh?"

No one said anything.

"I *said*, pretty bright, huh?"

Still silence from my companions.

I turned around and was surprised to find looks of horror on all three faces.

"Max?" Lefty, cried, staring hard at me, his eyes practically popping out of his head.

"Max—where are you?" Erin cried. She turned to April. "Where'd he go?"

"I'm right here," I told them. "I haven't moved."

"*But we can't see you!*" April cried.

HORRIBLE HISTORIES
History with the nasty bits left in!

The Awesome Egyptians
by *Terry Deary* and *Peter Hepplewhite*

The Awesome Egyptians gives you some awful information about phabulous Pharaohs and poverty-stricken peasants – who lived an awesome 5,000 years ago!

Want to know:
* which king had the worst blackheads?
* why some kings had to wear false beards?
* why the peasants were revolting?

In this book you'll find some foul facts about death and decay, revolting recipes for 3,000-year-old sweets, how to make a mean mummy, and some awful Egyptian arithmetic.
History has *never* been so horrible!

The Terrible Tudors
by *Terry Deary* and *Neil Tonge*

The Terrible Tudors gives you all the grizzly details of Tudor life for everyone – from cruel kings and queens, to poor peasants and common criminals.

Want to know:
* some terrible Tudor swear words?
* about terrible Tudor torture?
* why Henry VIII thought he'd married a horse?

Read this book to find some foul facts, some horrendous beheadings, a mysterious murder, some curious quizzes and gruesome games.

History has *never* been so horrible!

True Horror Stories
by *Terry Deary*

A chilling collection of terrifying tales that each claim to be true, presented by Terry Deary in all their spine-chilling reality. But, is there a plausible explanation . . .?
A whole village of people disappears without trace, and all anyone saw were strange lights in the sky.
An Egyptian mummy, disturbed after thousands of years, leaves a trail of horrible disasters.
Consider the facts and decide for yourself whether each gruesome story really is true – but keep the cover firmly closed once darkness falls, or your dreams could turn into NIGHTMARES . . .

True Monster Stories
by *Terry Deary*

Incredible? Impossible? Too awful to imagine? But someone, somewhere at some time has sworn that each of these strange stories is true . . .
Read accounts of the Yeti, the vampire, and less well-known beasts, like Black Dog and Mogawr; consider the facts and decide for yourself whether these monster stories really are true. And even if you choose not to believe, beware! These tales may linger in your thoughts and darken your dreams . . .

You Be The Jury
by *Marvin Miller*

Did Mr Rogers fake his burglary to claim the insurance money?
Is Stanley Woot's last will and testament a fake?
Did John Goode shoot his business partner by accident – or was it attempted murder?

Ten intriguing courtroom mysteries are played out before you. Examine each case, study the evidence, then make your decision. The final verdict is up to you!

You Be The Jury II
by *Marvin Miller*

Here we have twenty more intriguing courtroom mysteries for you to solve.

Which one of the identical Lee twins vandalised Farmer Foley's chicken coup?
Did Brenda Taylor deliberately set fire to her jewellery shop so she could claim the insurance money?

Examine each case, study the evidence, then make your decision. The final verdict is up to you!

You Be The Jury III
by *Marvin Miller* illustrated by *Harry Venning*

Order in the Court!

The court is now in session and *you* are the jury!
In these ten mysterious cases *you* must examine the evidence, *you* spot the clues, and *you* decide the verdict – guilty or not guilty.

You Be The Detective
by *Marvin Miller*

Can YOU solve the crime?

Seven baffling crimes have been committed, and YOU are the detective. You have to visit the scene of the crime, question the suspects and piece together the clues.

Who Dunnit?
by *Marvin Miller* illustrated by *Harry Venning*

A brilliant book for all budding detectives, with picture puzzle crimes to solve, a complex collection of codes to crack, hints on how to search for clues – in fact, everything you need to become a supersleuth.